Don't miss Jenna Mindel's delightful Regencies!

Kiss of the Highwayman

"A surprisingly tender love story."
—*Romantic Times*

Miranda's Mistake

"Another fabulous story from Miss Mindel, the queen of romance. Her tale of love has a wonderful plot, desire, and a longing ache for true love to conquer." —*Under the Covers*

The Captain's Secret

"Secrets, traitors to the crown, action, and danger add up to one of the most delightful books I have enjoyed this year! Very highly and thoroughly recommended!" —*Huntress Book Reviews*

Labor of Love

"A delicious blend of gentle humor and poignant heartache." —*Romantic Times BOOKclub Magazine*

Blessing in Disguise

"A delightful romance . . . [a] true reading pleasure."
—*Jo Beverley*

"Warm, witty, and deliciously romantic—a splendid debut!" —*Gail Eastwood*

SIGNET

REGENCY ROMANCE
COMING IN FEBRUARY 2005

Miss Whitlow's Turn

Jenna Mindel

A SIGNET BOOK

SIGNET
Published by New American Library, a division of
Penguin Group (USA) Inc., 375 Hudson Street,
New York, New York 10014, USA
Penguin Group (Canada), 10 Alcorn Avenue, Toronto,
Ontario M4V 3B2, Canada (a division of Pearson Penguin Canada Inc.)
Penguin Books Ltd., 80 Strand, London WC2R 0RL, England
Penguin Ireland, 25 St. Stephen's Green, Dublin 2,
Ireland (a division of Penguin Books Ltd.)
Penguin Group (Australia), 250 Camberwell Road, Camberwell, Victoria 3124,
Australia (a division of Pearson Australia Group Pty. Ltd.)
Penguin Books India Pvt. Ltd., 11 Community Centre, Panchsheel Park,
New Delhi - 110 017, India
Penguin Group (NZ), Cnr Airborne and Rosedale Roads, Albany,
Auckland 1310, New Zealand (a division of Pearson New Zealand Ltd.)
Penguin Books (South Africa) (Pty.) Ltd., 24 Sturdee Avenue,
Rosebank, Johannesburg 2196, South Africa

Penguin Books Ltd., Registered Offices:
80 Strand, London WC2R 0RL, England

First published by Signet, an imprint of New American Library,
a division of Penguin Group (USA) Inc.

First Printing, January 2005
10 9 8 7 6 5 4 3 2 1

Copyright © Jenna Mindel, 2005
All rights reserved

 REGISTERED TRADEMARK—MARCA REGISTRADA

Printed in the United States of America

PUBLISHER'S NOTE
This is a work of fiction. Names, characters, places, and incidents either are the product of the author's imagination or are used fictitiously, and any resemblance to actual persons, living or dead, business establishments, events, or locales is entirely coincidental.

To Viola Mindel

Thank you for all the goodies and cupcakes that helped get me through this book. And most of all, thank you for being my very special grandma who still likes to slide down the hill. I love you.

Prologue

December 1819

George Clasby slapped his friend Lord Ashbourne upon the back. "Congratulations, you dog." Ashbourne had just announced that he and his lady-wife were in the family way. The guests cheered and everyone was happy in love. Everyone, that was, except for him.

George breathed in the smell of fresh evergreens that had been gathered that morning. The women, alternating between song and laughter, had decorated every corner of the room in honor of Christmas. He sat next to a well-banked fire that crackled and hissed, adding a warm glow to the festive mood, but George did not feel much like celebrating.

He fingered his goblet of mulled wine and felt sorry for himself. Why had he let himself come to this pass? At thirty-three years of age, he already regretted the choices he had made, the life he led. He glanced across the room in time to see Harriet

Whitlow take a hearty bite into a tartlet. He had always thought her pretty, but she was as untouchable as the moon. Her usually pale complexion had turned rosy from the spiced wine that flowed as freely as the laughter surrounding him.

Bitter dissatisfaction twined in his gut as he watched couples that obviously enjoyed their state of wedded bliss take turns under the mistletoe. Lord Cherrington and his tall bride of less than six months kissed longer than George considered necessary.

The statuesque couple stood in the entryway and their heads nearly knocked the ball of white flowers off its anchor. The bride's parents, and hosts of the house party, merely encouraged the pair each time the kissing bough swayed.

The sight did not mix well with the flavorful wine. George had not found true love. In fact, he doubted he would ever be allowed the chance. That grim outlook made his spirits sink even further.

"Here now, Cherry, give Artemis some air already," Ashbourne yelled. "Let someone else have a go. Clasby, you've not been under the kissing bough and it grows late."

George looked at his friend of nearly five years. "There is not an unclaimed maid who'd be given leave and you know it. Besides, you have all wed!"

"That has never stopped you before," Ashbourne teased.

George tipped his glass and downed the last of its contents. "Very well, line them up and I shall kiss each and every one. A token of goodwill and appreciation for being invited to this fine gathering of friends and family."

Ashbourne laughed. "All but one. I will not allow my fair madam-wife into your clutches lest you make her swoon."

George knew better. Ashbourne battled a jealous temper that could hardly withstand the sight of his beloved kissing another. But the other ladies gladly joined the line. Lady Rothwell and her daughter, Artemis—now Lady Cherrington—stood under the lavishly beribboned kissing bough waiting for a quick buzz from the notorious George Clasby.

It was rather pathetic, George thought. He felt like a circus attraction. Each married lady giggled and carried on about kissing him. And then Harriet Whitlow stood before him with a soft smile and pink cheeks.

Miss Whitlow was highly respected among society. She was kind and conducted herself with complete decorum at all times. She was the epitome of prim and proper. But tonight she looked at him with a mischievous gleam in her eye. George nervously glanced toward her father, Lord Whitlow, who remained deep in discussion with Lord Rothwell, no doubt concerning prime horseflesh.

"Do not say that only married ladies may enter this line," Miss Whitlow said. Her voice was low, breathy, and completely at odds with her modest looks.

George's ears grew warm and his cravat suddenly felt tight around his neck. "Of course not."

He bowed, then drew her close, but his attention strayed toward her father.

She smelled curiously fresh, like the outdoors mixed with cinnamon and oranges. Her fine eyes sparkled and he realized for the first time that they were a lovely shade of gray. And then she lowered her heavy lashes.

George gently placed his puckered lips on hers for nothing more than a peck of a kiss, when her mouth opened. Surprised at her response, he closed his eyes and pulled her closer. His lips automatically moved softly against hers and he expertly teased her with his tongue. She hesitated only a moment, and then she followed his lead.

Unwanted heat seared his midsection and he forgot that he was in the middle of a drawing room filled with guests. He also forgot that he kissed a paragon of virginal morals and deepened the kiss, drinking in the luscious taste of her.

He heard the taunts and whistles of those gathered round and he pulled back immediately. "Happy Christmas, Miss Whitlow," he said quickly. His breath came heavy.

"Happy Christmas to you," she whispered. Her lips were swollen and her eyes were glazed in a dreamy sort of way.

It took considerable effort on his part not to pull her back into his arms for a second helping. He could hardly believe that an innocent such as she could kiss like a fiery angel. His lust was dampened completely when he noticed the terrible scowl on her father's face; Lord Whitlow had seen them.

George gave a quick nod to the angry man and then a short bow to his daughter and quickly excused himself to the refreshment table.

"Oh, well done," Ashbourne said.

"For a fool perhaps." George lifted the ladle from the crystal punchbowl and filled his glass. "Did you see the expression on Whitlow's face? Another moment under that kissing bough and I'd have been called out or worse."

"Oh come now, 'tis Christmas. *Even you* must be allowed a friendly kiss from a fine young lady."

George nodded as he drained his cup, but the comment did not sit well with him.

Even you . . .

When had he become so repulsive to polite society? He had made a mull of his good name without paying the least bit of attention. At first he had thought it merely fun and games. A married lady of nobility had tempted him as a young man and he thought no harm would come to him if he were discreet. Then the few lonely wives of the *ton* that he had gladly comforted turned into scores and pure folly.

He was, in every sense of the word, a rake. And no decent woman would ever willingly take such a libertine for a husband.

Chapter One

March 1820

*H*arriet sat in the window seat of her bed-chamber. She drew her knees close to her chest, rested her chin on top, and gazed out the window to the nearly empty street below. She wiggled her bare toes and let out a heavy sigh. She was back in London for her third Season!

She wondered if Mr. Clasby had any idea how she felt toward him. *Probably not.* She sighed again. *How pathetic!* When it came to Mr. Clasby, she was afraid of her own shadow. It had been two years since she first met the gentleman and yet she had done nothing to make him aware that she existed. She did nothing but yearn in silence while he entertained matron after matron.

She had kissed him under the mistletoe, but he had not appeared the least bit moved. It had taken three cupfuls of mulled wine for her to gather the courage to join the line of ladies waiting to kiss him.

And she had put everything she felt, hoped, and

dreamed for into that kiss. Afterward, Mr. Clasby had proceeded to treat her as he always had, with polite friendship, as if nothing had passed between them. She supposed a holiday kiss under the influence of mulled wine could hardly be construed as passion, but hers had been real. She was not the same after that kiss. Everything for her had changed into a new urgency to capture Mr. Clasby's heart once and for all.

She settled more comfortably against a cushion and opened her favorite book, Sir Walter Scott's *Ivanhoe*. She needed to think on something other than George Clasby, but in no time the words blurred before her eyes.

She had been through this before: the parties, the presentations at court, the dinners, and the balls. Each year her father chose a different gentleman for her to marry, and each year she had rejected them with the knowledge that she wanted the only man who did not want her in return.

She clasped the leather-bound novel to her chest and closed her eyes, recalling every detail of Mr. Clasby's lips upon hers. His lips were surprisingly soft and gentle. The warmth of his mouth and the dizzying sensation of his tongue against hers were things she would never forget.

"Oh!" she whispered with a groan. "How can he remain so indifferent toward me!"

That one kiss had effectively shattered her world. She was convinced that this, her last Season, might be her only chance to do something about Mr. Clasby—something more solid than her urgent prayers.

She had always prayed for Mr. Clasby to fall in love with her. She also prayed for his soul, but figured that if he would just love her, then eventually his soul would fall into place as well.

The apparent fact that their kiss meant nothing to him proved how much he needed her. He needed a woman of character to reform him. George Clasby was a rake. Not a hardened rake, not even a cruel rake, but a man completely given over to his sinful pleasures.

He had lost all sense of real affection. She had read it in his eyes countless times over Christmastide as he moped about Rothwell Park. She simply had to save him. She cared for him far too much to let him waste into an old lecher.

She tossed her book aside. How could she hope to read when the image of Mr. Clasby danced through her thoughts? He was not the most handsome man she had ever seen, but she did indeed have a weakness for his thick, dark red hair that waved softly away from his forehead. His ruddy coloring gave him a robust, healthy appeal compared to many paler gentlemen. And his eyes, goodness but his eyes were the color of shining copper. She sighed yet one more time.

The opening of Almack's was but two days hence and she had to figure out how she would act when she saw Mr. Clasby again. What was she going to do?

"Harriet?" Her father opened the door and then peeked his head into her bedchamber.

All thoughts of Mr. Clasby scattered when she heard his voice. "Yes, Papa?"

"Might we have a coze before the whirlwind of a Season is upon us?"

"Of course." Harriet made room for her father to sit next to her on the window seat.

He clasped his hands in his lap and looked terribly serious.

Harriet touched her father's elbow. "What troubles you?"

"Harriet," he started. "After the last two Seasons, I have begun to wonder if you will ever seriously consider becoming mistress of your home."

With a familiar sinking feeling, she knew where her father was headed. Season three and still unwed. Every gentleman he had picked out and paraded before her was of sterling character and reputation—all near perfect in their appearances and proud bearing. But not one of them needed her, nor wanted her for anything more than to bear his heirs.

Her father refused to understand where her heart lay, and to be fair, she was too afraid to tell him. She had held out for the attentions of one man for two years now. This was, in all seriousness, her final chance to secure the affection of Mr. Clasby. But she must tread lightly where her father was concerned.

"Of course I have thought about it." She stood and walked to the fireplace, concentrating on the flames licking the lumps of coal.

"At your come-out, you were young and a little shy. But after a bit of town bronze, you had scores of gentlemen vying for your attention and a couple for your hand. But no one met with your approval."

"Papa." Harriet turned around. "I loved none of them."

"Perhaps you did not give them a fair chance."

Harriet remained quiet a moment and studied her fingernails. Dare she mention Mr. Clasby as her reason? Last year when she worked up the courage to name him as a possible suitor to test her parents' reaction, her father nearly had an apoplexy.

Her father walked toward her and lifted her chin. "Harriet, my dearest girl, as much as we would like to keep you with us, you are dangerously close to being considered on the shelf. There are worthy men of moral character who need a strong and capable girl like yourself to take to wife."

Harriet smiled. Her parents were dear, and her father was, unfortunately, correct. She was twenty-one, very soon to be twenty-two. Another Season on the Marriage Mart would be embarrassing in the extreme.

"Point taken, Papa," she said.

"I want my daughter wed to a good man, and I'll not accept no for an answer this year. Your mother wants a grandchild and there is no hope in sight of such a thing from your brother."

Harriet laughed, but inside she cringed. How unfair that she was expected to marry before she reached the ripe age of twenty-two. Her elder brother by three years was free to extend his travels on the continent and take as long as he pleased to consider choosing a bride.

"Are we understood?"

"Yes, Papa." Harriet conceded.

"Very good. Tonight we dine with the Duke and Duchess of Harrowby. Dress with extra care, my dear."

"I will." She had tried to sound interested but her voice fell sadly flat.

Her father kissed her nose and pinched her cheek, then left.

Harriet wandered along her room and her attention was caught by the Bible on her bedside table. She ran her fingers over the sturdy cover. Their curate at home had always preached that the Lord helped those who helped themselves.

It was one of the views her father had been so proud to share with his man of the clergy. The mighty Lord Whitlow was an active man who did not laze about. He believed God blessed men, whatever their station, if they labored in some capacity and kept their minds sharp.

She slumped back onto the cushioned window seat. She knew in her heart that if she were to have any chance of capturing the interest of the man she loved, she must *do* something about it.

Perhaps she should go to him. But how? Even if she succeeded in capturing his attention, her father would never approve of the match. Well, that she must leave in the hands of God. If God answered her prayers, He would surely take care of her father's stubbornness.

*   *   *

George whistled as he dressed for his club. He was a man with new purpose and he had never felt more lighthearted. He had done a lot of thinking since Christmas. He wanted what the others had—Ashbourne and his lady-wife, even Artemis and her Lord Cherrington. George wanted to find love. Real love, not the sham he had been engaged in for years of lustful pleasures. But first his sadly ignored image needed to be improved.

He had decided to reform his reputation as a licentious rake starting this Season. He wanted to find his very own true love yet he had no hope of meeting this girl destined to hold his heart if he could not garner invitations to the same functions as she.

Over the last few years he had gradually been left off guest lists. If he did not take drastic measures to prove to the *ton* that he was willing to change, he might be left on the fringes of society forever. Now was the time to act if he had any hopes of sealing a happy future for himself.

If all went as planned, doors once opened but now closed might be reopened to him. Eventually he could entertain options of courting any number of decent young ladies of noble birth and character. He knew that society might very well reserve judgment on his changes until next year. But in his mind, anything worth having was worth waiting for. At least that was what his father had always said to him as a small boy.

True love had to be worth the wait, but regardless, something had to give. He could no longer face the lonely life of playing cicisbeo and more to unhappily married ladies of the *ton*.

To prove he was indeed serious, he had recently refused the advances of the luscious Lady Ellerton, wife of the conveniently absent Lord Ellerton. George was quite proud of himself. Lady Ellerton was not only divine in proportions, but she was something of an intellectual as well. It took considerable strength of his newly found character to turn away from all that she had promised. Whatever discomfort he must endure this Season would be worth shaking the empty feeling that had gripped him these past six months.

"Will that be all, sir?" his valet asked after tying a near perfect cravat in the Mathematical.

"Indeed." Clasby nodded before placing a rakishly angled beaver hat atop his head. "Tell Mrs. Sweet that I shall dine at my club."

"Very good, sir." His valet was not pleased that George had brought the frumpy housekeeper from his country estate to Town.

George felt it necessary to add the respectable Mrs. Sweet to his nearly all male staff. Besides, her presence was a reminder of his goal. She had been in the employ of his mother when she was alive. George could hardly carry on his rakish ways under the nose of Mrs. Sweet.

In moments, he was out the door of his town house, which was situated on the north edge of Mayfair. The early spring air was mild, so he did not mind the long walk to arrive at Boodle's in time to order a leg of lamb for his supper.

After he had vanquished his appetite for food,

he settled into a chair near the window and lit a cheroot with a fully whetted appetite for gossip. He needed to know more about who made their come-outs this year.

"What news, Clasby!" Jory DeVillars said from the nearby billiard table. "You were not in Town over the holiday."

"No, I was not." George brought his cheroot to his lips for a deep pull and then he exhaled a long tendril of smoke. "I rusticated at Rothwell Park over Christmastide."

"And you arrived late to Town, my friend. Any trouble?" DeVillars took his shot, sending a ball into the desired pocket.

George shrugged. "No trouble. I've just been thinking that I need to change my ways."

"'Pon rep, do not say you're joining the Methodists!"

"I doubt I'd sit here puffing away if I were." George chuckled. "Besides, you know that I cannot abide church services. Join me for a brandy and tell me the latest *on-dits*. I heard the king finally stuck his spoon in the wall, but that is all I know of it. Was there a large funeral?"

"Indeed there was." DeVillars, along with two others, sat down. DeVillars ordered another bottle and brought George up to date.

After an hour or more of laughter and scandalous tales, Sir Frederick Welton, Freddie to his friends, cleared his throat. "I have heard that Miss Whitlow has returned for her third Season."

"Why can't the gel settle on a husband? She does not lack for offers," DeVillars said.

"Is she some kind of bluestocking?" Freddie asked. "I see her often at Mr. Smith's Bookshop."

"She is pretty as a daisy, but her father is overly protective," DeVillars said. "Lord knows I never made the cut."

"As if she'd have you," George added to guffaws of agreement from the men around the table.

"My sister heard that Whitlow is hoping for success with the new Earl of Grafton," Freddie said. "Grafton has finally come into the title from his departed sire, and he has come up to Town with his pockets very warm indeed. The ladies are abuzz with curiosity like bees over a honeypot. He is hailed as something of a paragon of virtue who neither plays deep at cards nor drinks much at club."

"He's never kept a mistress, either," DeVillars said with a sly wink. "A prerequisite for her father, I think."

"Good luck finding a man such as that," George said with a derisive snort.

"Hey," Freddie interjected.

"I beg your pardon, Sir Welton." George made a mock bow. "You are nearly as virtuous as you are inexperienced."

"Now see here!" Freddie stood, then sat back down when another bottle of brandy was delivered.

Envy that Grafton could so easily have his pick of young ladies smote George's heart. Miss Whitlow was a charming girl. And she did kiss rather well. He clearly remembered how pliant she had been in his arms. But then again, due to the holiday cheer, they had all drank deeply from the bowl of mulled wine. In truth, she was as religiously proper as Lord Grafton sounded. They would no doubt make a perfect match.

An idea dawned on him. "By Jove, that's it!" he hissed.

"What's that, old boy?" DeVillars asked.

George merely grinned. The very solution to turning about his reputation as quickly as possible was as plain as daylight to see. Miss Whitlow was the answer to his current trouble. She was good *ton*, perhaps even better than that. He needed some of her high standing in society to rub off on him. If he were to respectfully pay court to her, he might yet be saved.

He took a drink of his brandy and rubbed his chin. He had stumbled upon a very good idea indeed. And since another man was her intended, that made it all the more perfect. Lord Whitlow would never allow George Clasby serious pursuit of his daughter, but perhaps he would allow friendly calls if George were upfront from the very beginning.

Miss Whitlow would hardly entertain false ideas where he was concerned. With a pattern-card of perfection like Grafton begging at her heels, he doubted Miss Whitlow would give him a second thought. It is not as if they ever cared for one another more than having friends in common.

George took another deep pull of his brandy, draining the glass. "I believe I might pay a call upon Miss Whitlow."

"*You?* Court an innocent?" DeVillars asked.

"There comes a time when a man must think of his future," George said. When the men continued to stare at him as though he had just grown a second head, he added, "Comforting dissatisfied matrons has quite lost its appeal."

"You haven't a chance with Miss Whitlow when compared to Lord Grafton," Freddie said.

"And therein lies the beauty." George drew another cheroot from his coat pocket.

Harriet had taken her father's advice, or rather, his directive. She dressed with utmost care and consideration. Her terribly straight and fine hair had been arranged perfectly into a riot of curls that would no doubt fade and flatten before the end of the night.

The light blue Swiss muslin gown with a silver net overlay was cut in the latest style, with long sleeves that had been gathered all the way down her arms. Diamond drops hung from her earlobes and a simple necklace of silver cord adorned her neck. White gloves covered her hands that gripped the railing as she descended the stairs.

"A pretty picture you make, Harriet." Her father bowed to her.

"Thank you, Papa."

"He will be quite impressed, I think," her mother said softly.

"Who?" Harriet asked.

Her father gave his wife a sharp look.

"No one in particular, dear," her mother hastened to add.

It did not matter. Her father had always pushed

gentlemen her way. "Matchmaking again, Papa?" Harriet asked.

"There will be a few gentleman present this evening that I wish for you to meet."

Harriet nearly rolled her eyes, but instead she smiled and held out her arm. There was no sense in making a fuss about such things. If she were to escape this Season unscathed and matched only to Mr. Clasby, she needed to step softly near her father. Her mother, she knew, wished only for her happiness. Had it not been for her mother's calm intervention, Harriet might have been married off her first Season.

"Very well, Papa," Harriet said with false bravado. "Let us go and meet these fine gentlemen."

The drive belonging to the Duke and Duchess of Harrowby was lined with carriages. The intimate dinner with friends her father had described sadly resembled a crush. A slight tremor of nerves fluttered down Harriet's spine. She supposed she should be accustomed to such lofty company—her father was a peer of the realm with vast connections. Still, the fact remained that she became anxious in such excruciatingly high circles.

The haute monde expected her to behave with the perfect manners befitting her station. Even so, she had her own image of character to uphold and her parents were proud of her prudence. She was a reflection of them. Regardless of how well she carried herself, the least little slip of her tongue or drop of her napkin was remarked upon. It was unnerving in the extreme and she never had grown completely comfortable in such surroundings.

She gave her pelisse to the footman and waited with her parents and several other guests yet to be announced by the butler. She scanned the ballroom filled with lords and ladies and diplomats. Mr. Clasby would never have been invited but still she searched the crowd for him. Much to her disappointment, she did not see his dark red head, nor did she see her friend Artemis and her husband.

Finally, the Whitlow family was announced and they descended the few steps leading to the ballroom into a throng of people. Harriet nodded toward acquaintances and stopped to chat with the few ladies she called friends. She had just begun to relax and enjoy herself when she felt a tap upon her elbow.

"Harriet dear, there is someone I would like you meet," her father said.

With a sinking feeling, she turned to face a handsome gentleman wearing an expectant expression.

"Lord Grafton, allow me to present to you my daughter, Miss Harriet Whitlow."

Lord Grafton took her hand. He bowed and let his lips just barely brush her gloved hand. "Miss Whitlow, I am honored."

Harriet realized that she should say something. She was slightly surprised by the man's appearance. He was tall, had dark hair, and was indeed pleasantly formed. "Lord Grafton," she finally said. She caught her father looking pleased. This was the gentleman picked out for her this year.

"I have heard many good things about you," Lord Grafton said.

"Have you?" Harriet took his proffered arm. She spied her father sneaking away from them with a delighted wink of the eye.

"Indeed. Surely you are aware of the high regard you are given by members of society. But you are truly more beautiful than I had heard."

Harriet had the grace to blush. She knew she was considered quite pretty by many but his flattery lacked genuine conviction. "Thank you, my lord."

"Your father quite sings your praises."

"As he should," Harriet said with a small laugh. "He is, after all, my father, and desperate to be rid of me."

It was Lord Grafton's turn to laugh and Harriet had to own that she rather enjoyed the sound. His voice was deep and clear.

The Harrowby butler opened the double doors that led to an enormous dining room.

"Come," Grafton said. "Supper is about to be announced. You must sit by me."

"But Her Grace may have other seating arrangements," Harriet said quickly.

"Then we shall switch them."

Harriet knew her fate was sealed. Lord Grafton was going to be her supper partner whether she wished it or not. "Very well."

They entered the dining room to find that the

Duchess of Harrowby had in fact placed Lord Grafton and Harriet conveniently next to each other. Harriet smelled the distinct odor of her father's machinations at work; he was not a man of subtlety. He wished for her to wed a desirable *parti* and evidently he had found such a man in Lord Grafton.

Harriet cautiously took her seat, but her appetite waned. Lord Grafton appeared to be a self-assured man confident in obtaining his quarry, and Harriet had been hand-delivered with her father's stamp of approval.

She slipped off her gloves and laid them in her lap, underneath her napkin. If ever there was a time for her to learn a little boldness, it was now. She had to think of a way around of this chain of events, else she would no doubt end her Season trussed up and wed to Lord Grafton.

Chapter Two

*H*arriet entered Almack's Assembly Rooms and her stomach churned in anticipation of seeing Mr. Clasby. It was opening night and it seemed the entire *ton* was in attendance—so many notable figures milled about. After the somber death of the king in January, society was ready to indulge in the frivolity of a Season. Candles shimmered from the many chandeliers and the orchestra played softly from the balcony, but it was not yet time to dance.

Harriet was early, she knew, but she did not wish to miss a chance of running into Mr. Clasby. Her parents had obliged her by arriving early and she was grateful. She never cared to be fashionably late as was the trend. She felt like she had missed something when she arrived late.

She looked around for the telltale reddish hair that was Mr. Clasby's. He had always attended Almack's and she fervently hoped that he would do so again this year, unless the patronesses decided Mr. Clasby's reputation had become too much for the matchmaking mamas who subscribed.

She dashed into the room set aside for the ladies' privacy and quickly checked her image in the mirror. Her carefully constructed upsweep of ringlets had just barely made it through the fine mist outside. Wispy tendrils of straight hair were already falling from her pins, but there was nothing to do for it now. She pinched her cheeks to bring out some much needed color and with a deep breath, she stepped back into the crowded assembly rooms.

"Miss Whitlow." Lord Grafton came toward her and bowed. "You look divine this evening."

"Good evening, my lord," Harriet said with a distracted air. Lord Grafton blocked her view of the main entrance.

"If I may, do you have your card ready?" he asked. "I must be assured of a dance."

Harriet produced her card. She nearly groaned when Lord Grafton scrawled his name across two places, both waltzes. She had hoped to save one for Mr. Clasby, if he ever arrived. *How perfectly predatory,* she thought. Lord Grafton was intent on making his interest known. But that was how the game was played, so she could not fault him for acting as expected.

Lord Grafton was not an annoying man. He was arrogant to be sure, but then he was an earl. She knew that several ladies would gladly trade places with her regardless of the way Lord Grafton held his chin—slightly raised in haughty disdain of the world around him. It simply would not do if she sulked or gave Lord Grafton too cool of a reception. Her father would be deeply disappointed in her if she treated the young lord with anything other than courtesy. There was no harm in being polite, but she refused to encourage his suit.

"Do excuse me, Lord Grafton," she said. "I find that I am in need of refreshment."

"Let me escort you, my dear." He held out his arm.

Harriet took it stiffly. He did not act familiar or warm and yet he used the endearment as if that should bear account to his purpose of courting her. She felt a little sorry for the man. He certainly was not accomplished in the art of flirtation. But then neither was she. Not that she wished for him to flirt—on the contrary. She wondered if perhaps Lord Grafton did not feel the need since her father obviously approved of him.

She accepted the cup of weak lemonade Lord Grafton offered and took a deep sip before they moved close to the edge of the grand ballroom floor. She was indeed parched and emptied her cup completely.

She scanned the room once again until dark red hair caught her attention. The gentleman was indeed Mr. Clasby. Her insides fluttered and she felt terribly unsteady, as if she had experienced a sudden shock.

She had been trying to prepare herself since Christmastide for this first meeting after the holiday party, but all was lost as she looked at him. She felt excited and scared to pieces all at once, with no hope of remaining calm.

She watched Mr. Clasby's broad shoulders move confidently through the crowd. He bowed and nodded cheerfully to various acquaintances. And then he turned, looked directly at her, and smiled. Harriet shuddered and her heart beat so hard she thought for sure Lord Grafton could hear it. She managed a weak smile in return, but Mr. Clasby had already moved along his merry way.

She realized with deep disappointment that what she had already suspected was true. He had given her no look filled with longing. In fact, there was no clue that he even remembered their holiday kiss. Mr. Clasby reacted as if nothing out of the ordinary had ever transpired between them. She let out a disappointed sigh.

"Are you acquainted with Mr. George Clasby?" Lord Grafton's voice intruded on her thoughts.

Goodness, she forgot completely that he still stood next to her. Harriet felt her cheeks blaze. How long had she been watching Mr. Clasby's every move under the watchful eye of Lord Grafton? "We have mutual friends in common," she said as a matter of fact.

"He is a libertine and a rake." The displeasure in Lord Grafton's voice was quite clear.

"So it is said, but I believe he is an honorable man beneath the devil-may-care façade."

"Madam," Lord Grafton said, horrified. "Perhaps you mistake the meaning of the word *honor*. George Clasby is far from its reaches."

Harriet winced, but turned to face him. How dare he insult Mr. Clasby! Did he even know him?

"Lord Grafton," she said lightly. "I am well versed in the meaning of honor."

Lord Grafton had the decency to bow his head, though he did so stiff as a board. "I meant no offense, Miss Whitlow. I am surprised you count the man as one of your acquaintances. My sincere apologies if I have offended."

Harriet nodded uncomfortably. "Of course, your apology is well received and appreciated, my lord."

Fortunately, Harriet was saved the need to speak further when several gentlemen approached to reserve dances upon her card. Each man cast a quick glance toward Lord Grafton, who continued to hover nearby, announcing to one and all that any fellow interested in courting Harriet Whitlow had very strong competition.

George signed his name on as many young misses' cards as their mamas would allow. It pricked his pride to have several ladies demurely pull their cards back after receiving a frown of disapproval from their sponsors. One of the young ladies who denied him was a tempting morsel with shining black hair and eyes. She, and others like her, were prime examples of why he had to remain on his course of action.

Even so, he shrugged off his first failure. He was in the process of making reparations; he could hardly expect the desired change to manifest itself overnight.

Finally, he made his way toward his goal, Miss

Harriet Whitlow. He must be seen dancing with her this evening to start the *ton* tabbies talking about what he might be up to. He came up behind her. "Good evening, Miss Whitlow."

She turned quickly as if startled and then blushed profusely. He thought the heightened color of her cheeks suited her, since her complexion was normally quite pale.

"Mr. Clasby," she said in that deep breathy voice he admired.

Then he noticed the tall wall of body belonging to Lord Grafton standing next to her. "Grafton." He looked up into dark, disgusted eyes. "How are you this fine spring evening? My deepest condolences on the passing of your father."

"Clasby." The man literally looked down his patrician nose.

George ignored the offensive lord's rude reception and tended to the business at hand. "Miss Whitlow, might you spare a dance for me?" he asked. It was dashed uncomfortable to make his request under the stern gaze of Lord Grafton. Poor Miss Whitlow. The man acted more like her guardian than an amorous suitor.

"I would be honored," she said quickly with marked inflection upon the word honor. "In fact, if your first dance is not spoken for, I believe the orchestra is warming up for a quadrille. We can approach the floor since other couples are already forming their sets."

"Miss Whitlow, I am entirely yours," he teased with his arms spread wide. He thoroughly enjoyed the affect his gesture had upon Grafton,

whose chin jutted out with irritation. Clasby
chuckled under his breath.

He could not say that he blamed Lord Grafton.
Harriet Whitlow was a fine young woman if one
wished to court and marry a saint. She was well
known to attend the Church of England regularly.
She dressed with extreme modesty that bordered
on dowdiness and although sweet-natured and
charming, she was a tad retiring. He had never
known her to voice an opinion.

But she kissed like an angel, he thought quickly.
Indeed that was true. He looked at her a little
more closely. Might there be fire underneath her
stiff high collar? If so, Grafton was in for a pleasant surprise. Perhaps Miss Whitlow might melt
away the icy edges of the haughty young lord.

Clasby held out his arm to Miss Whitlow and
said, "Lord Grafton, please excuse us."

Once they were in the center of the ballroom
amid the other dancers, Miss Whitlow whispered
shyly, "Thank you for asking me to dance, Mr.
Clasby."

" 'Tis my pleasure." He held her hand and
bowed as the music swelled.

Her pretty gray eyes twinkled with merriment
and her smile widened. She was very taking when
she smiled.

They came together and linked arms to twirl. "I
see Grafton is among your suitors this year," he
said. "He is a grand gentleman with much to rec-
ommend him."

"So I have heard from many, but we have only
just met," she said with that seductively deep

voice. Her voice did not match her prim exterior one bit.

"You could do far worse," he added just before they turned to face the other dancers in their set.

"Perhaps I could do much better," she said breathlessly.

"I don't see how. He's considered this year's prime catch."

She took his hand. "As if I care for those things."

George moved diagonally to twirl another lady. When he returned with Harriet in place, he asked, "And what is it that you care for, Miss Whitlow?"

"Many things and many people."

"Ah, a wise answer and yet you give nothing away. This is your third Season and still you have not made a choice." He whirled her around.

"Why must I?"

George smiled. "Why indeed."

She glanced at him shyly. "What of you?"

"I hope to wed someday, if I am fortunate enough to meet the right lady."

Her eyelids closed and he noticed the thickness of her lashes. "Then let us hope this is your Season. For finding the right lady, I mean."

"Indeed. Let us hope for the both of us." He twirled her about again and the quadrille came to an end. He escorted her toward a gentleman waiting patiently. "Your next partner, perhaps?" he asked softly.

"Yes. Thank you, Mr. Clasby."

"Your servant, Miss Whitlow." He left her in the hands of a young gentleman of very modest means, but Miss Whitlow smiled just as warmly to him as any other gentleman. George watched as she took to the floor with the young man for another country-dance. She moved with utmost grace, and the charity of her kindness toward the empty-pocketed young man was not lost on him.

He congratulated himself on the wisdom in choosing Miss Whitlow to call upon. Although they had friends in common, he would not mind claiming her as a friend of his own. He had never believed men and women could be friends, but something about Miss Whitlow's demeanor told him that she would indeed be a good friend to have.

He wondered why she had not appeared enamored of Lord Grafton. Other than her kindness, she did not wear her emotions upon her sleeve. Even so, Lord Grafton was surely handsome to any young lady's eye. But he imagined that Miss Whitlow was not one to be taken in by appearances alone.

He had known her for nearly three years and in all that time, she had never acted impulsively or foolhardy. She was a steady person who obviously thought things through. She would not jump after a man, not even one as fine as Lord Grafton. Miss Whitlow had far too much character for that.

Just then George noticed Lord Whitlow's scowling countenance bearing down on him. He needed to speak with him if he had any hopes of calling upon his daughter this Season. Cautiously, George made his way through the crowd until he stood before the stern visage of Lord Whitlow, an admirably built man who had remained fit—and forbidding.

"Lord Whitlow," George started. "I wonder if I might beg your ear a moment."

Lord Whitlow's eyebrow arched. He was indeed an intimidating force to behold.

George loosened his cravat as if it had suddenly become tight. He coughed and then rephrased his request. "I wish to discuss a matter of some importance." He held up his hand to keep Whitlow from walking away from him. "After you hear me out, you will understand why I did not approach you at your town house. Might we find someplace private?"

"Very well." Whitlow gestured for George to lead the way.

With Lord Whitlow following close behind him, George walked into the room reserved for the tables of refreshments. He politely offered the other man a cup of lemonade, then poured his own cup and took a deep breath. "As you may know, I have complete and utmost respect for your daughter." He glanced at Lord Whitlow, whose scowl deepened even though his interest was obviously piqued. George forged on. "I wish your permission to call upon Miss Whitlow, not for the purpose of offering for her but rather in an attempt to salvage my sore reputation." There, he had said it straight out.

"Your intentions?"

"Honorable, I assure you." George looked around to check that no one overheard the conversation. "I did not wish to seek you out at home else it may have been construed as a desire to offer for her hand. I do not wish to mislead anyone. Miss Whitlow and I are merely friends and my hope is to remain so."

"Why my daughter?" Lord Whitlow took a sip of his lemonade. To any passerby, they looked as casual as if they spoke of the weather.

George chose his words carefully. "Miss Whitlow is the most respected young lady in Town, perhaps in all of England. I am weary of the life I have led and one day I wish to marry, but I cannot hope to find a decent lady who would have me as I am. I must improve my reputation or I am doomed. If allowed to join Miss Whitlow's callers, with your approval, of course," George nearly stuttered, "my actions would be proof of my desire to reform. I shall not get in the way of a match with Grafton, I assure you."

Lord Whitlow digested the information carefully, taking time to think before answering. Finally he said, "My daughter is not to be trifled with. Should you lead her astray or play her false, you will answer to me, Mr. Clasby."

George felt a nervous shiver pass down his spine. He had heard the stories of Lord Whitlow's past. He was something of a rakehell who had dueled often, leaving a string of broken hearts and injured opponents on the field. Some said he had even killed a man or two. Even though Lord Whitlow had reformed his ways, he was an imposing figure nonetheless and not one to be trifled with.

"I give you my word," George said. "No harm

shall befall your daughter. I will not play the paramour but continue in an honest friendship under your advisement at all times."

"Even so, I should like to consider your request further."

"Understood, my lord. Shall I call upon you for your final answer?"

"Indeed. Come tomorrow." Lord Whitlow stalked away.

George breathed easier. His course was set and he felt like an enormous weight had been lifted from his shoulders. Of course, Lord Whitlow may yet refuse, but George believed that *perhaps* was as good as *yes*.

Gingerly, he made his way back to the main ballroom where he perused a line of young ladies who were making their first bows to society. He noticed a particularly luscious young miss with curves that could not be hidden under the white muslin gown she wore. Without hesitation, George approached one of the patronesses of Almack's for an introduction.

"What are you about, Clasby? Miss Trelling is an innocent young lady," Lady Cowper said with amusement.

"Exactly so. I would hardly ask if she were not," he said with a wink.

"Leaving behind your lecherous ways are you?" Lady Cowper leaned close. "I heard about you refusing Lady Ellerton. Good show, young man. She would have ruined you."

"A new Season, a new life," he chirped. The beautiful Miss Trelling spoke to another gent.

Even from a slight distance it was clear the young puppy tripped over his tongue, and he stared so intently at the beauty's charms, George feared his eyeballs might pop out of their sockets at any moment.

"Come with me," said Lady Cowper.

He followed as she interrupted the young fellow and made introductions. Then Lady Cowper acted as an angel of mercy and took the stammering young man along with her. George had the delicious Miss Trelling to himself.

"Good evening." He bowed.

"Indeed. Thank goodness Lady Cowper intervened. I could hardly understand the man. Tell me, Mr. Clasby, what brings you to London?"

George stepped back. Miss Trelling's manner was far too direct. Even so, he would not pass up the opportunity to partner her delectable form upon the dance floor. Too bad this was opening night, he thought. More than likely, Miss Trelling had not been given permission to waltz. "Do me the honor of allowing me to reserve a dance upon your card."

"There are two spaces without names, Mr. Clasby." He did not mistake the disappointment that touched her voice when she repeated his name. She produced her card and smiled, yet no warmth reached her eyes. Obviously she looked for a title.

He quickly scratched his name next to a quadrille and bowed. "Until then," he said politely, but realized he had a daunting search ahead for a lady worthy of his true love.

*   *   *

"Did you enjoy your evening?" Harriet's father asked once they were in their carriage.

She yawned before answering. "I did." The carriage swayed as they rounded the corner onto Piccadilly.

"I noticed that you danced with Mr. Clasby."

Harriet's back stiffened and she braced herself for a scold. But none came. Cautiously she said, "We are friends, Papa," which was indeed true. He had always treated her in a friendly manner. "Mr. Clasby was at the Rothwell hunting party the last two years as well as their Christmas gathering. We are bound to attend the same parties. I cannot in good conscience snub the fellow."

"Nor would I ever ask you to do so. Simply have a care where Mr. Clasby is concerned." Her father's voice was soft but his expression was stern and completely serious. "He may be among your callers tomorrow, if I allow him to stay. You will let me know if he acts improperly toward you."

Harriet's breath caught in the throat. She felt like throwing her arms around her father's neck for a strong embrace, but she held back. She could not show the excitement she felt. Her father might actually permit Mr. Clasby to call; she dared not hope for anything more just yet. With a quick prayer of gratitude heavenward, Harriet took a deep breath and said, "I promise that I will, Papa."

She glanced at her mother who lightly shrugged

her shoulders, but added a comforting wink. It was the slightest change in her father's behavior, but even so, it was a start and Harriet was ecstatic.

"Thank you for giving Mr. Clasby permission to call." Lord Whitlow's wife slipped into bed. "Harriet is thrilled. It appears that finally the young man has realized what a treasure she is."

Lord Whitlow shrugged his shoulders and grumbled, "We have as good as encouraged her, you know."

"You know as well as I which way the wind blows with our Harriet. 'Tis time we see what depth there is in her feelings. We should at least give the fellow a chance. I hear he is trying to mend his ways."

"Prue, please." Lord Whitlow climbed into bed next to his wife. He hoped he had done the right thing, but only time would tell. That and the truth behind George Clasby's request. "The boy came to me and asked permission to call for reasons other than courtship."

His wife sat straight up. "Whatever do you mean? Did he ask for permission to pay his addresses or not?"

"It was not like that. Clasby is indeed trying to mend his ways. He believes that if he is seen in Harriet's company, his reputation will improve as it most assuredly would. He vowed that his intentions are in the name of friendship only. He has no designs upon our girl."

"Oh dear," his wife sighed. "Harriet has nursed

a *tendre* for him for the past two years. What if she truly comes to love him, Farley? I will never forgive myself if Harriet's heart is broken."

He slipped his arm around his wife's shoulder. "Come now, Prue. Harriet is much too smart for that. She will come to see Clasby for exactly what he is—just a man with a foul past who must prove himself serious in his efforts to reform. I have heard it bandied about at my club that he refused Lady Ellerton's advances, so I believe the boy means business about repairing his name."

"Hmmm. He deserves a chance for happiness with our Harriet. She might be just what he needs." His wife cast her huge blue eyes upon him. "Farley, you must also put the fear of God into Mr. Clasby. If he causes our daughter pain, he will rue the day he decided to single her out!"

Whitlow chuckled. "I cannot help but think that half of Clasby's allure is that up until now, he has been forbidden fruit. Besides, he cannot outshine Grafton. Perhaps if Harriet is given the chance to see each man on equal footing, so to speak, she will come to see that Grafton is the man for her."

His wife gave him a look he had seen dozens of times over the years. She clearly thought his logic slightly flawed, but then she had been after him to get to know Mr. Clasby for two years. Now was the time. "We shall no doubt find out in time." She leaned close to kiss his cheek.

"Here now. Of course we shall." Lord Whitlow blew out the candle on the bedside table before nestling close to his wife. She was the love of his life and she knew a thing or two about human nature. But he did too and was convinced that once Harriet realized Grafton was the better man, they'd have nothing to worry about: she'd leave this nonsense of mooncalf love for Mr. Clasby behind.

Chapter Three

The following morning, Harriet pulled her dearest friend, Artemis, into the cozy breakfast room. "Finally, you have come to Town! I have been waiting an age to see you." She gave her a quick squeeze. "I thought you'd never get here. Your letter said you planned to arrive in time for the Season, not after it had already begun."

With a laugh, Artemis returned the embrace. "'Tis Cherry's fault entirely that we are late. There was so much that needed to be done at Cherring House—we have been making improvements since we wed."

"And you still look very happy." Harriet stepped back to look at the friend she had not seen since Christmas. She pulled the bell rope to order tea.

"I am deliriously happy." Artemis twirled until she fell into an overstuffed chair.

"We have so much to discuss. I am simply bursting to tell you," Harriet said.

"What pray?"

"Mr. Clasby requested a dance last evening at Almack's and my father did not raise a huff! In fact, he is allowing him to call."

"Truly?" Artemis did not look excited but rather wary.

"I know, I know." Harriet waved her hand in dismissal before she gave their housekeeper instructions for tea. She quickly sent her on her way so they might continue their conversation privately. "Do not let my hopes run too high."

"Harriet," Artemis began. "You once gave me very sound advice to steer clear of unsuitable gentlemen. You cannot think your father will ever approve of Clasby. In fact, I am not quite sure I approve of him for you."

Harriet knew her friend meant well, but even so the remark stung. "Artemis, do you truly know him?"

"No, but—"

"There, you see." Harriet was quick to point out.

"Harriet," Artemis warned. "He has a reputation for dalliances with married ladies."

"Of course, I know that. He needs to find real love, Artemis. I am sure that once he does, he shall change."

Artemis did not look convinced. "Why Clasby? What is it about him that has you so moved? You can easily have your pick of pleasing gentlemen."

The tea tray arrived and once again, Harriet politely sent the housekeeper away. Harriet concentrated on pouring tea before answering.

Softly she asked, "What was it that drew you to Lord Cherrington?" She handed a dish to Artemis and before her friend could answer, Harriet plundered on. "I do not know, really. Who knows why a person finds another intriguing. Perhaps it is all because of the kindness I see in him. At my first come-out, I was quite terrified." Harriet poured a dish of tea for herself, adding sugar and milk. "I had just received my vouchers and it was the opening night at Almack's. I knew no one and felt certain I would be ill, I was so very nervous. Mr. Clasby was the only gentleman to take pity on me. He fetched me lemonade and made me sit before I swooned. He then proceeded to tell me any number of humorous stories until I laughed and quite forgot my jitters. Soon, several gentlemen requested dances and my evening was saved from disaster."

"And you have had a *tendre* for him ever since?" Artemis plucked a biscuit from the tea tray.

"Shamefully, yes. I knew he was not the type of man I should care for. I am not stupid. I have heard the whispers of his paramours and assignations with married ladies of the *ton*. But I cannot believe that sort of behavior makes him happy." She sighed heavily, then took a sip of her tea. "One look into those copper-colored eyes of his and I was quite lost." Harriet took another sip.

"Poor Harriet."

"Poor me, indeed. He treats me with utmost respect and *friendship*. More's the pity."

"What if that is all he ever offers you—his friendship?"

"I do not know. All I know is this year, I must at least make him aware of my feelings and hope to win his favor. This is my last chance. My father has Lord Grafton picked out for me and I may find myself wed regardless. My parents insist on seeing me settled."

"They will marry you off just like that?" Artemis snapped her long fingers.

"Let me see." Harriet rested her chin in the palm of her hand. "This will be the third Season I have refused every eligible gentleman approved by my father. Yes, I do believe they just might."

Later that afternoon, the Whitlow drawing room was filled with gentlemen. Harriet had danced with many of them the previous night and each one vied for her attention. Some had brought her posies, some read sonnets devoted to the color of her eyes or hair, and some paid their compliments quickly and left to visit other drawing rooms.

Lord Grafton was there too. He stood apart with a haughty expression of ownership that Harriet could not like. He even remained longer than the usual quarter hour. Harriet smiled and chatted gaily, but inside her disappointment grew. Her heart had lurched each time a new arrival entered the room, only to be sadly discouraged when it was someone other than Mr. Clasby.

Just when Harriet was about to give up hope that Mr. Clasby would ever call, he finally arrived.

His smile was bright and genuine. Warmth washed over her, causing her to smile in return.

"Good afternoon, Miss Whitlow," he said with a bow of his dark auburn head.

She nodded calmly even though fireworks of excitement erupted inside her. "Mr. Clasby, how good of you to call."

"In the neighborhood, don't you know." He winked and took the seat nearest to her.

"Then I am indeed fortunate."

Harriet's mother entered with a tray laden with biscuits and sweetmeats. The housekeeper followed with tea.

Mr. Clasby was the first gentleman to his feet. "Lady Whitlow, may I assist you?"

Her mother did not appear the least concerned to see the subject of so many dire warnings in her drawing room. "Mr. Clasby," she said. "If you would be so kind as to pass the plate of biscuits."

"I would be honored, ma'am."

Harriet smiled as she watched Mr. Clasby offer the baked goods to each gentleman still present. It was a dream come true—Mr. Clasby had called and her mother looked almost pleased. She wondered what her father would have to say on the matter. No doubt she would hear that later.

"Mr. Clasby." Lord Grafton had come away from the wall and joined the flock of admirers. "I should like a biscuit, if you please. Do you pour tea as well?"

"Indeed, I am quite accomplished at serving tea," Mr. Clasby replied with good humor.

"You must have considerable opportunities to

practice your skills while in Town," Lord Grafton drawled with veiled meaning.

"Not so much any longer. My tea service has grown dull and tarnished from overuse. It needs a good polishing, but one day it will shine as good as new."

The few gentlemen remaining chuckled at Mr. Clasby's retort. Worried about the tension between the two men, Harriet looked from Lord Grafton to Mr. Clasby. She knew they spoke of Mr. Clasby's reputation, but a crowded drawing room was hardly the place to discuss it. She hoped the men would cease their banter.

"Some things can never be made new and clean again," Lord Grafton said with a sharp edge of disapproval. "But it grows late, and I must beg your leave." He bowed low over Harriet's hand and then proceeded to do the same to her mother. "Ladies, gentlemen, your servant." And then he left.

Harriet breathed a little easier.

"I beg your pardon, Miss Whitlow," Mr. Clasby said softly, for her ears alone.

"'Tis nothing." She waved her hand in dismissal of the subject.

"Ah, but I have arrived. That is cause enough to raise a few feathers, I am sure." He winked at her once again.

Warmth flooded her insides. She knew her cheeks were pink but it did not matter. Surely her prayers were being answered. Mr. Clasby had come to her. She need only do her part and make him aware that she more than welcomed his attentions. How she would do that was something of a mystery, but she would find the answer in due time.

The rest of the gentlemen took their leave one by one until only Mr. Clasby remained. Harriet glanced at her mother, playing chaperone, who sat on the far settee attending to her needlework as if nothing was out of the ordinary.

"It appears that my time has also come to an end," Mr. Clasby said as he stood.

"Indeed." Harriet felt terribly self-conscious with her mother nearby.

"I must ask," he said, then hesitated. "Would you care to take a drive in Hyde Park, say an hour from now?"

Harriet was speechless. She looked at her mother.

"You may go with Mr. Clasby," her mother said.

"Unless of course, you have made other plans," he added when still Harriet had not spoken.

"No . . . no. I would like that above all things."

"Very good." He bowed. "I shall return and collect you with my curricle." He turned toward her mother. "Lady Whitlow, an enchanting pot of tea. I thank you."

"You are welcome, Mr. Clasby. And if you need help cleaning your tea service, do bring it by the next time. The Whitlow household is well versed in making things new again, as long as you promise to have a care once it is polished."

"Your offer of aid is deeply appreciated." He bowed. "Ladies, your servant. Until later, then."

Once he left, Harriet turned to her mother.

"Mama, whatever has changed your mind to allow me to drive out with Mr. Clasby?"

Her mother hesitated before she finally answered. "When Mr. Clasby arrived, he asked permission to take you about during the fashionable hour. He is a dear friend of Lord and Lady Ashbourne and the Rothwells. Since we have just spent the holidays in their company, your father and I decided we did not wish to insult them by refusing acceptance of Mr. Clasby's calls. And he considers you a *friend*, my dear."

Her mother's emphasis on the word "friend" was not lost on Harriet. It was a word she was beginning to loathe when used in the same sentence with Mr. Clasby.

"And what was all that talk of tarnished tea services?" Harriet spread her arms akimbo.

Her mother came close and took both of her hands. "Harriet," she started, "there is something I feel you must know."

The look of concern on her mother's face caused a sinking feeling in the pit of Harriet's stomach. Something was indeed wrong. "What is it?"

"Mr. Clasby approached your father last night at Almack's."

Her heart soared. Could it possibly be that his intentions were for spring nuptials? She nodded for her mother to go on since she did not trust herself to speak without cheering for joy.

"Harriet, dear, I know you care for this man, but you must understand that Mr. Clasby is calling upon you in order to improve his reputation."

Harriet sat very still as her mother's words sank

in with harsh reality. He had no intention of offering for her, he simply wished to serve his own purposes.

Her mother softly caressed Harriet's cheek. "I am so very sorry sweeting, but I wanted you to know so that you may remain levelheaded throughout the coming months."

"Of course, Mama." Harriet firmly pushed aside her disappointment. "Why else would he call? We are indeed friends, and as a friend, I will help him restore his name. At least this is a start in the right direction. He is making a change."

George pulled his curricle up to the curb in front of the Whitlows' town house. He got down and flipped a coin into the hands of his tiger to hold the reins. His matched pair of bays swished their black tails and threw their heads in impatience for having stopped.

"There, there," George soothed the eager horses. "We'll be on our way soon enough." He had to own that he too looked forward to the drive. Miss Whitlow had always been pleasant, and the idea of an hour spent in her company was not unwelcome.

He felt a prick at his conscience for using her and her influence to better his reputation. He'd like to count Miss Whitlow a friend—perhaps having friends in common was more the case, but even so, he'd bet a monkey that if he asked for Harriet's help directly she would not hesitate to give it.

Asking her to help pull him up from his self-made mull of a reputation in order to one day court another paid her no compliments. He had gone through her parents to allay their concerns, but he was not proud of it.

But sometimes one must do the uncomfortable when trying to improve oneself, George thought. Which included bearing Lord Grafton's acid tongue. He hoped Miss Whitlow had paid little heed to Grafton's remarks at tea. The man had rubbed salt into an already gaping wound. Lady Whitlow knew, though, and George was grateful for her kind response. It gave him hope that he was on the right track.

He took the steps two at a time, adjusted his cravat, and lifted the heavy wrought iron door knocker that hung from an ornate lion's mouth. The pounding reverberated through the wood door and in no time the Whitlow butler was ushering him into the entry and then the drawing room.

"Mr. Clasby," the butler announced in a monotone.

Miss Whitlow jumped up from her seat and walked toward him before her parents even rose from the settee. "Good afternoon, Mr. Clasby. How good of you to take me for a drive."

" 'Tis an honor. I owe my gratitude to your kind parents for allowing it." George did not mistake the raised eyebrow of Lord Whitlow. The man's eyes were clear, and in them George read a strong message of warning. Lady Whitlow merely smiled and bade them both a good time.

George offered his arm to Miss Whitlow, and

for the life of him, he could not recall ever feeling this nervous before. As she wrapped her arm around his, he may as well have escorted a maid formed of spun glass. One slip, one wrong move, and she'd shatter and all his hopes for restoration would fall to the floor with her. He cleared his throat. "Shall we go?"

"Indeed."

They silently made their way outside to his carriage. George did the pretty and helped Miss Whitlow into her seat.

"Comfortable?" he asked. He climbed in just as his tiger hopped onto the ledge at the back of the carriage.

"I am. This conveyance is quite nice."

"With a fresh coat of paint in honor of this year's Season." He took the reins in his hands and they were off.

"No wonder it shines." She looked anywhere but at him.

"Er, yes." George wondered why there was awkwardness between them. They had never carried on this way before, but then they had only ever chatted briefly at various parties and balls. They had been archery teammates at breakfasts and the like, but their camaraderie had always been practiced in a group. This was the first time they had ever been alone.

The scent of orange blossoms tickled his nose, tempting him with the memory of how nicely Miss Whitlow kissed. He ran a finger around the knot of his cravat. His valet had tied the dashed thing too tight. "How is your Season progressing this year?" His voice sounded a bit shrill and he nearly winced.

"It has only just started. If you can consider a third Season fine at all, then 'tis fine."

"Ah yes, another Season." George did not wish to share that many had in fact remarked upon it.

"This will be my last, I assure you," Miss Whitlow said with a slight smile.

"Then I wish you all the best."

"Thank you, Mr. Clasby. I shall endeavor to make it the best." She looked up at him and for a moment he studied her face.

She truly was pretty. He wondered why he had never looked closely before. Her features were delicate but well formed, her small straight nose leading to near perfect bow-shaped lips. With complete clarity, he remembered kissing those lips and warmth flooded through him. His reaction was to be expected, he supposed, since he had chosen celibacy this Season. Nothing could interfere with what he needed to do, especially not thoughts of Miss Whitlow's luscious mouth.

"What are your plans for this Season?" she asked with an earnest expression.

"My plans?" He focused on the road as he took a turn and entered Hyde Park.

"I saw you dancing with many young ladies at Almack's. You did not once enter the sphere of a married woman."

George felt his cheeks coloring. Of course she would know about his dalliances. He had danced attendance upon many a *ton* matron for years now. She had probably witnessed his fawning adoration a time or two. He found that thought distasteful. Harriet Whitlow should not even know of such things! But she did, and she was waiting for him to answer. "I am trying to put that behind me."

"Turning over a new leaf?"

"Something like that." George glanced at Miss Whitlow and caught the smile on her face just before she looked away.

"I am very glad to hear it. May I ask what has prompted you to attempt the change?"

George shifted uncomfortably. What should he tell her? He hoped to find his true love once he was respectable enough to pay court to her once he found her? "I began to feel that the life I led was an empty one."

"I can quite understand how it would pale eventually," Miss Whitlow said. "My father was a rake in his day until he fell in love with my mother."

George nodded. Yes, that was what he was hoping for.

"So you see?" said Harriet. "It can be done. My father has been completely faithful to my mother all these years."

George had not even considered that part of his improvement. He had never thought beyond finding his true love. Could he be faithful? He hoped so. Even so, this could not be an appropriate conversation. "I thank you for your encouragement, Miss Whitlow."

"You are most welcome." She smiled sweetly and added shyly, "If I can be of any help in your endeavor, please do not hesitate to ask."

"Your company helps my cause a great deal," he said.

She tipped her face up toward the sun and exclaimed with sheer pleasure resounding in her deep voice, "It is a beautiful day, is it not?"

Since the weather was so mild, he had left the leather hood down. He took notice of more than the warm sunshine beating down upon them. Her enjoyment lightened his spirits. She was a dear lady and a pretty one to boot.

"Yes," he finally agreed. "It is a glorious day." He broke into a smile of his own.

They made their way toward Rotten Row. The sandy track quickly filled with various carriages of the *ton's* fashionable wishing to see and be seen. In moments, the haute monde would recognize just who sat prim and proper next to him. If Lord Whitlow allowed him to escort his only daughter, then surely others would soon follow suit. In time, his name would be back where in belonged—in the annals of high society.

He slowed the horses to barely a walk as he took his place in line. He enjoyed the surprised looks upon several faces when they saw Harriet Whitlow in his carriage.

Miss Whitlow smiled, nodded, and demurely waved at acquaintances and friends alike. Her responses did not change in manner or tone. She was friendly and polite to one and all—even the mushrooming upstarts who were obviously no more than fortune hunters.

They stopped for a moment so that Miss Whitlow could ask one particularly empty-handed fellow about his mother's health.

After they had moved on, George said, "May I compliment you on your graciousness?"

She turned in her seat to face him. "Mr. Clasby, whatever for?"

"That man you spoke to with such a sweet smile is a well-known fortune hunter."

"Of course he is. He hasn't a choice, really. His father speculated in a shipping deal that went terribly south. Lord Lazenby's estate is sadly entailed and in desperate need of repairs. His mother has not moved into the dower house and she suffers from the desire to have a disease. He must find a well-dowered lady to set things to rights and I cannot say that I blame him."

"I did not realize," George said.

"Of course not. 'Tis not something a man bandies about, you know."

"So how did you come upon this information?"

"Ladies talk, Mr. Clasby. I attended the academy with his cousin. She made her come-out last year."

"Indeed," he murmured. Miss Whitlow was as knowledgable as she was well-connected.

They proceeded slowly amid the other carriages. George grew tired of the constant smiling and nodding when he spotted Lord Grafton riding alone on horseback. Something about the man set him on edge and it was not simply Grafton's comments regarding the irreparable damage done to his reputation. He rode a horse well, sitting high and straight in the saddle. He was the very picture of elegance. Miss Whitlow was sure to notice.

Grafton brought his horse next to the carriage. "Miss Whitlow, good afternoon."

"Good afternoon, Lord Grafton," she said.

"Clasby, what a surprise." Grafton addressed him as an afterthought, his eyebrow arched with condescension.

"Indeed," he managed through clenched teeth.

"Miss Whitlow, the sun pales in comparison to your beauty. That frock is positively stunning."

George coughed to keep from uttering a sarcastic remark. He had not noticed what Harriet wore, but when he looked closely, he found it particularly unremarkable. Harriet's loveliness shone from her decency, not from the dress she wore. *What a pompous chub!*

Miss Whitlow smiled. "Thank you. But your flattery is surely exaggerated as this gown is quite simple."

"I am indeed earnest with my compliment," Grafton said with brevity. "Simple or not, it becomes you."

"In regards to simplicity, Lord Grafton is an expert." George relished the chance to give the man a verbal jab.

Grafton cast him a glance that would no doubt wither a lesser man. George did not care to impress Lord Grafton, nor did he value the man's opinion. If anything, he wished he would go away.

"Since, as Mr. Clasby said, you are an expert,

then I gratefully accept your kind words," Miss Whitlow said with a demure nod of her head.

Egad, but she was polite! She had just spoiled his fun.

"Miss Whitlow." Grafton bowed. "Your servant." And then he moved on.

"Jackanapes," George muttered under his breath. Fortunately Miss Whitlow did not hear him because she was hailed by another carriage. George had promised Lord Whitlow that he would not interfere with Grafton's courtship. And he was determined to keep that promise, even if he did not like the man one whit.

Chapter Four

*H*arriet had promised to meet Artemis for a morning ride in Hyde Park. They had made their plans when Artemis had called, and Harriet was looking forward to sharing every tidbit of her outing with her friend. She approached Artemis, who sat perched upon her mare. "A fine morning, Artie," Harriet said as she reined in her mount close to her friend. "It promises to be another beautiful day."

"Indeed it does," Artemis said with a smile. "Are there new developments with Mr. Clasby?"

Harriet had much to tell. "Yes. Mr. Clasby called on me yesterday afternoon while I received other gentlemen. Afterward he asked permission to drive me about in his curricle during the fashionable hour."

Artemis' eyebrows rose in surprise. "Your parents allowed it?"

"They did. Mama said that they did not wish to insult your family or Lord and Lady Ashbourne by refusing his presence, but then Mama explained the real reason Mr. Clasby has chosen to call."

"And what is that?"

"You see, Mr. Clasby is trying to redeem his reputation. Since I have plenty of respectability to share, he asked my father if he might call on me with the purpose of improving his image."

"Oh, Harriet, I am dreadfully sorry."

She held up her hand to stop the flow of unwanted pity from her friend. "Please do not feel sorry for me. At first I was stung by the news, but there is hope. Mr. Clasby admitted to me that he wishes to change his ways and I believe he means it. This way, I have the chance to spend time with him and hopefully make my feelings known."

Artemis cocked her head. "You needn't be so resigned to fate about it. Perhaps you should do a little wooing of your own. Who says we must leave these things up to the men?"

"Indeed, but what can I do?"

"What did you do when you kissed Clasby under the mistletoe?" Artemis asked.

"I joined the line and asked for a kiss," Harriet said. "But that was entirely different circumstances. It was a holiday and besides, I felt emboldened by the mulled wine."

Her friend gave her a pointed look. "Yes, but you did not leave things to chance then. Why do so now?"

"I have been thinking along those lines for days, but I must bolster my courage. My largest obstacle at the moment is Lord Grafton. He believes, no doubt due to my papa, that his way is clear. The arrogant look upon his face when he spotted me next to Mr. Clasby was insufferable. He cannot care for me in the least—he hardly knows me. He doles out flattery that is not genuine by half. Why is it that he chooses to annoy me when Mr. Clasby has finally made his appearance?"

Her friend laughed.

"'Tis not amusing, Artemis. I am truly perplexed. There are numerous appealing and well-dowered ladies on the mart this year. Why me? I am nearly on the shelf, as it were."

Artemis became quite serious, even though her eyes sparkled with mischief. "Because, my dear Miss Harriet Whitlow, Lord Grafton is a fastidious man who wants only the purest, most modest young lady to produce his heirs. Something about securing good behavior and decorum in his offspring. That most revered lady in London is you."

"How do you know this?" Harriet asked.

"Cherry overheard Grafton saying as much at his club."

"My goodness." At least Harriet knew the why of it, even though she found such knowledge an example of how society rarely accepted a person for *who* they were but rather *what* they were.

"Shall we ride?" Artemis asked.

"By all means, yes." Harriet did not wait another moment. She clicked her crop lightly upon her gelding's backside and away they went, following Artemis at a spanking pace toward the sandy track of Rotten Row, nearly vacant due to the early hour of the morning.

As she galloped around the track, what Artemis had said continued to plague her. Lord Grafton had no intention of getting to know her as a person. He wanted her merely for what she represented in the eyes of the *ton*.

For once, she wished she were not so highly regarded. But then she halted her complaints and counted her blessings instead. Had she not such a sterling reputation, Mr. Clasby would not have sought her out. It was often said that God worked in mysterious ways. Perhaps Artemis had the right of it.

The Lord helps those who help themselves. Harriet clearly remembered the curate from home speak those words to his congregation. Harriet believed it was time to take his advice and act.

Harriet walked through the huge drawing room in Lord and Lady Collington's Kensington home. Lord Grafton hovered nearby, rambling on about his county seat in Sussex until Harriet was nearly sleepy-eyed. She did not wish to be mean-spirited, but the man had asked nothing about her. He had not once asked after her hobbies or interests. Instead, he droned on about how thrilled she would be with his rose gardens. Did he even know if she liked roses? For shame, their scent made her sneeze. Did he once consider thinking about that?

"Once again, your gown is divine in its modesty, Miss Whitlow," Lord Grafton said.

Harriet looked down to check which gown she had chosen to wear this evening. It was a simple evening dress of pale pink with a high neck and long sleeves that had been gathered every two inches by fabric rosebuds.

"Thank you, my lord," she finally said. She looked about the vast expanse of the room. Must she remain with him all night? He had escorted her and her parents in his closed carriage due to the slight drizzle that had started late in the afternoon. Considering the distance, Lord Grafton must feel her constant presence was payment owed to him.

"Good evening, Miss Whitlow," George Clasby appeared from out of nowhere. "And of course, Lord Grafton."

"Clasby," Lord Grafton drawled.

"Mr. Clasby, I did not realize you were coming tonight." Harriet tried to pull her arm out of Lord Grafton's clasp, but to no avail. The dratted man held her firmly. And he positively glared at Mr. Clasby.

"Yes, well, Collington and I were at Cambridge together. Friends, you know."

"That accounts for the invitation," Lord Grafton drawled.

"Indeed. It is rather nice to have friends," Mr. Clasby retorted.

Harriet could tell Mr. Clasby wanted to say more, so she intervened before the two men squared off. "I quite agree, Mr. Clasby. I am heartily glad to see you here."

"Thank you, Miss Whitlow, charitable as always." Mr. Clasby bowed but he looked angry. The tops of his ears were red. "Your servant." And he went on his way to speak to other guests.

Harriet watched where he went, his dark auburn hair easy to spot as he bowed and scraped over several ladies' hands. Even with his touchy reputation, he was received by many. A few sticklers snubbed him outright, but he accepted it calmly.

He turned then and caught her watching him from across the room and her face grew hot. He looked embarrassed too, and her heart went out to him. It must not be easy to be looked down upon. She gave him what she hoped was an encouraging nod, even though she wished he would stop paying attention to other ladies.

Lord Grafton was at her elbow all evening with a possessiveness she could not like. At this rate, Mr. Clasby would think her hand spoken for before she had a chance to share her true feelings or win his heart. Something must be done and she must think of it quickly.

Dinner was announced and gratefully, Harriet was placed next to someone other than Lord Grafton, but he was not far away from her. Neither was Mr. Clasby. When she listened closely, she could hear both men's conversations.

Mr. Clasby was animated, often bringing gentle laughter to his listeners. Lord Grafton spoke of serious matters, the death of King George III and the implications for society of the Prince Regent being crowned king.

The course of her life stretched out before her. If she married Lord Grafton, her life would lean toward a serious contemplation of the world and the raising of Grafton heirs. She would have to impress the haute monde, and Lord Grafton would require complete respectability and decorum from her at all times.

Should she share a life with Mr. Clasby, she could venture into obscurity and spend the rest of her days choosing whether to go to Town or stay at home or visit Artemis and Cherry. Laughter would be their mainstay, she was sure of it, and their children would grow in merry surroundings with only the responsibility of making what they wished out of their lives.

She glanced at her parents seated further down the large dining table. Her father had such high expectations for her, and Lord Grafton was at the center of his wishes. Could she truly turn down her father's choice yet again, with the paltry excuse that the man was pompous?

She could imagine her father's censure. *Of course he is pompous. He is an earl. Earls are expected to behave with a measure of arrogance, my dear.*

She wished Lord Grafton would give up his pursuit and look elsewhere for a bride to birth his heirs! She wanted none of it.

She glanced at the object of her thoughts. Lord Grafton desperately tried to ignore the lady seated on his left. The lady was none other than Lucinda Bronwell, last year's reigning Incomparable. She was a dowerless girl on the hunt for a man of wealth who would be so dazzled by her looks that they would forgive her family's dour finances. Her beauty was matchless, and her gown was cut on the edge of indecency.

Harriet nearly giggled as she watched Lord Grafton ineffectually end each conversation that

Lucinda had started. The girl was a trifle bold but the *ton* accepted her outré behavior simply because of her stunning beauty.

Last year, she had fallen into the Collingtons' pond without a chemise under her gown. When she emerged, several gentlemen received an eyeful of her nearly naked charms. Instead of being completely ostracized, the fickle *ton* sympathized with whispers of "the poor girl, penniless, don't you know." It was beside mentioning, lest one be criticized for chastising the unfairly favored beauty.

Lord Grafton wore an expression of stern disapproval every time Miss Bronwell moved forward to allow him a glimpse of her full bosom, which got Harriet to thinking. She mentally reviewed every gown in her hanging wardrobe—all of them decorous. Perhaps it was pride on her part that she refused to lure a gentleman, even Mr. Clasby, with her rather modest physical attributes.

Perhaps therein lies the key to her troubles. If she could repel Lord Grafton, it would be well worth it. If more daring gowns attracted the attention of Mr. Clasby in the process, then so much the better. Time was of the essence and she could ill afford her own sensibilities or pride. She too had changes to make.

Several days passed and although Mr. Clasby had called on her, she knew he had called on several other young ladies as well. She had heard his name mentioned often among the ladies she joined to take tea or go shopping.

With her own gentlemen callers besieging the

drawing room, Harriet was unable to spend any quality moments with Mr. Clasby, and Lord Grafton's presence was constant. She had also attended balls and parties to which Mr. Clasby had not been invited, much to Harriet's disappointment.

Even so, Mr. Clasby was a common topic of discussion. The consensus was that he was indeed looking upon the marriage mart for a possible bride, but most were a tad skeptical. Not everyone believed Mr. Clasby to have the resolve to change his ways. The gossips eagerly awaited his fall and subsequent return to clandestine affairs and meetings with married ladies of society. The gossip columns had diminished in length due to Mr. Clasby's crusade to respectability.

Harriet believed in Mr. Clasby, and today promised to be splendid since she knew he had received an invitation to the literary salon at Holland House honoring the works of the newly made baronet, Sir Walter Scott. Harriet had looked forward to the readings for weeks. Lord Grafton had again offered his escort and her parents had accepted his conveyance.

Harriet had been busy making over her gowns with the help of her seamstress. As she twirled before her cheval mirror, she was pleased with the results. Her décolletage was neither improper nor overdone, but her neckline was low enough to show the swell of her slight breasts. With a satisfied nod to her maid, Sally, Harriet turned to quit her room just as her mother peeked into her bedchamber.

"Lord Grafton is waiting, dear," her mother said.

"I am ready." Harriet held her breath as she waited for her mother's reaction to the changes made.

"You look lovely," she said.

Harriet breathed easier. Either her mother had not noticed or she was not going to make a fuss. Regardless of which, she was relieved. She snatched her reticule from her bed and followed her mother down the vast staircase into the drawing room where Lord Grafton and her father were in deep discussion.

Lord Grafton looked up when they entered and frowned deeply. His reaction to her appearance was all that Harriet had hoped for. He did not appreciate the visibility of her womanly charms one bit.

Holland House was a sad crush by the time they arrived. Lord Grafton escorted her mother, leaving Harriet on her father's arm as they walked up the steps.

"You changed your gown." Her father had noticed.

"Indeed."

"Might I ask why?"

"I grew tired of appearing the dowd."

"There is nothing wrong with modesty, my dear," he said and then sighed. "But I understand that ladies must also follow the fashions."

They left their pelisses, gloves, and top hats with a footman in the anteroom. Lord Grafton then held out his arm for Harriet to take and they entered the ballroom that had been converted to look like a theater. Several rows of chairs had been set up, the dining room doors had been opened, and the long tables were laden with various refreshments.

Harriet could hardly wait to see Mr. Clasby. She hoped that he would notice the change in her gown.

George moved through the crowd. He was grateful for the positive effects that calling on Miss Whitlow had already brought about. Invitations were slowly multiplying in number. Good invitations, too. By the end of the Season, his worries should be over.

The rest would be up to him. He had worried that it would be difficult to keep away from the allure of adulterous matrons, but he had been pleasantly surprised. He could not say truthfully that he did not long for his bed to be warmed by a willing woman, but something about his abstinence proved to be a cleansing balm. It reminded him daily that he was on the right course in life.

"Good evening, Mr. Clasby."

George turned toward the familiar voice and his gaze connected with the neckline of a gown that revealed a gentle swell of delicious white skin. He quickly looked up into the rainy gray eyes of Miss Whitlow. But he had to revisit her breasts peeping upward from the fabric that held them.

Her bosom was not large and the cut of her gown was completely acceptable, nearly modest, in fact. Still he was surprised to discover the lus-

ciousness of her form that until this night had
been completely under wraps.

"Mr. Clasby?" she said with concern.

"Uhhh, Miss Whitlow, forgive me. My wits
have gone begging, I'm afraid." He bowed and
felt the heat rising to his ears. Lud! He had ogled
her outright. Abstinence must have a stronger effect on him than he had originally thought.

"There is nothing to forgive. Now tell me, are
you a fan of Sir Walter Scott's work?"

"I cannot say that I am." George had never read
one of his books or poems.

"I am quite certain that after this evening's
readings you shall soon become one." She looked
incredibly pretty with soft wisps of her light
brown hair falling about her face.

"Perhaps you might sit next to me? If I have
questions, you, being the expert, can no doubt answer them correctly." He did not care that she
had arrived with Grafton. Tonight, he simply
wished to enjoy her friendly company. He was
not about to admit that he hoped to further enjoy
the view of her décolletage.

"I shall be happy to assist you."

"Miss Whitlow, what sweet words." George
winked at her and she responded with a soft
laugh. He enjoyed the soft pink color that stole
over her cheeks. He was sorely tempted to try to
deepen the tint, but thought better of it. Flirting
with Miss Whitlow under the very noses of her
parents—not to mention Lord Grafton—was not
wise in the least. What on earth was he about?

"Quickly, we must take our seats," she whispered. "The reading is about to begin."

George escorted her to the third row, not wishing to sit directly in the front. He knew she wanted to be close to the gentleman speaking so that she could hear clearly. But once they were seated, he wished they were as far back as possible.

The chairs had been placed so close that his thigh kept brushing against hers. Every move he made resulted in direct contact with her. It did not help matters that her perfume teased his nose. She smelled sweetly of orange blossoms. He leaned closer to inhale that scent once again, forcing himself to keep his chin up so that it was not obvious that he glanced at her bodice.

The creamy swell of her skin was a tempting sight, indeed. He did not wish to ignore such beauty, but he was not about to stare considering that many seated in the rows behind him would no doubt know exactly where his gaze traveled. He managed to keep his vision firmly fixed upon the gentleman reading, even if he heard little of what the man read.

Harriet's heart raced. There had been desire in Mr. Clasby's eyes—she would wager all her pin money on it! And now sitting next to him, the sensations that coursed through her when his thigh brushed against hers or his shoulder touched her own were indescribable. It was all she could do to concentrate; her insides were constantly aflutter.

Her parents sat only two rows behind them. She dared not whisper through the presentation, else she would have a peal rung over her ears when they arrived home. She quietly reached into her reticule and produced a small, sharpened piece of charcoal. She turned over her program, listing the various readings planned for the night, and wrote a short note for Mr. Clasby.

Well, what do you think? She gently nudged him.

The corners of his lips turned up and he took the paper and charcoal from her.

Of Scott or of you? he wrote.

Harriet's heart skipped a beat. She concentrated on breathing evenly, but panic took over with sharp claws that kept her from thinking rationally. What should she do? Dared she respond that she wanted to know what he thought of her? Goodness, whatever would he write?

In a moment of cowardice, Harriet wrote, *Why, Scott of course.* She immediately rued her action. She needed to make him aware of her interest and she had just let the perfect opportunity slip by. She was worse than a coward!

He scribbled back. *A trifle dull.*

Harriet's insecurity was momentarily forgotten. Her favorite author had just been maligned. She quickly scratched, *Dull? Are you mad?* and handed the paper to him.

Perhaps. He winked at her as he cautiously settled the paper and piece of charcoal onto her lap.

Harriet smiled. She could think of nothing more

to write—until it dawned on her. *Do you plan to attend the Waterton-Smythes' garden fête tomorrow?*

He reached over and scribbled on the paper still in her lap. *I do.* And then he dropped the charcoal on the floor and had to bend down to retrieve it. The warmth of him so close caused a shiver to rush up her spine. She felt strangely bereft when he leaned back against his chair, returned the charcoal to her, and placed his hands firmly upon his knees.

Harriet was about to respond with yet another note, but there was little room left, not to mention that she spied a glaring look from the elderly lady seated next to her. She quietly folded the program and tucked it back into her reticule along with the charcoal. She would keep the exchanged messages forever.

She was relieved that he would attend the garden party thrown by the Waterton-Smythes, the highest sticklers in Town. It was common knowledge that they had fallen on hard times. They had been forced to lower their lofty standards in the attempt to marry off their two daughters for wealth. Regardless of their straightened circumstances, they still viewed the rest of the *ton* with haughty eyes.

The eldest girl was the only one wed. She had recently married a rich nabob, their connections to the haute monde being the trade-off. The word being put around was that the man had actually softened his toplofty bride. The readings came to a close much too soon for Harriet, but she lingered close to Mr. Clasby. She did not want this magical evening with him to end.

"Shall we make our way to the refreshments?" He offered her his arm.

"I should like that above all things." Harriet looked around and spotted Lord Grafton in conversation with a couple of gentlemen near the back row of chairs. *Thank goodness*, she thought. She could make her escape.

Once they were both inside the dining room and seated at one of the scattered tables with their plates laden with food, Harriet asked, "Mr. Clasby, if you do not care for Scott's works of fiction, what do you like to read?"

"Miss Whitlow, I do not harbor an appreciation for fiction."

"You must like poetry then," Harriet said.

He made a face. "Can't abide it."

"Why Mr. Clasby, what *do* you read?"

He looked thoughtful. "I read and study publications that offer something to learn."

Harriet nodded. "Then you must read the Bible."

"Ah, no." His expression was of complete distaste.

Harriet felt a stirring of disquiet. "But you have read it."

"Of course, what schoolboy hasn't?"

He looked uncomfortable with her prodding questions and so she relented. She had assumed he was a well-read gentleman. It surprised her that he found little enjoyment in passing the time between the pages of a good book or at the very least, striving to better oneself by delving into the Holy Scriptures. "You are quite correct, sir," she said a little sheepishly.

"Come now, Miss Whitlow, chin up. You meant no offense." He reached across and patted her hand. "I am by no means an intellectual, but I do take an interest in history and even the current issues at Parliament. But even more so, I am fascinated by the inventions of our time. Hot air balloons, for instance. Who would have ever guessed that men would find a way to heat air until a stretch of fabric should make a ball that rises?"

"Indeed." Harriet stared into his eyes, captivated by the fervor in his voice. She certainly did not mind that his hand still rested upon her own.

"I shall tell you a secret," he whispered as he leaned closer.

Her head nearly touched his. "Yes?" she breathed.

"I have tinkered with some inventions of my own. Expansions upon already conceived modern advancements, really."

"Like what, pray tell?"

"At my country home in Derbyshire, I have used the very principles of a water closet and brought them into the bath so that I might stand and douse myself with water instead of always having to sit and soak in it."

Harriet felt her eyes widen as an image of a very wet Mr. Clasby flashed through her mind, making her wonder just what his broad shoulders would look like completely bare. "I should very much like to see that," she said quickly. "It must indeed be faster."

He chuckled before answering. "It is. I have yet to figure out how to heat the reservoir of water. My servants must add heated water to make it bearable."

"Why, Mr. Clasby, I had no idea you dabbled with science."

"Not exactly science. I simply like to know how things work. Besides, water closets are hardly the subject for polite conversation."

Harriet flushed with pleasure to be honored with the knowledge of his *secret* hobby. In her opinion, he should not be ashamed of such interests regardless of the impropriety of discussing matters that relate to the privy or personal hygiene.

She had thought Mr. Clasby a man devoted only to pleasure. Clearly there was more to him than she had realized. It only served to deepen her desire to know him better.

"Miss Whitlow." Lord Grafton's voice intruded. "I have finally found you."

With a start at his high-handed tone, Harriet straightened guiltily, as if she had been caught doing something wretched. Her cheeks turned hot and that merely served to deepen Lord Grafton's disapproving frown.

He glared at Mr. Clasby, who stared insolently back as if daring Lord Grafton to make an accusation.

Harriet needed to put things to rights without delay. "Mr. Clasby was just telling me about the advances of modern science." Her voice sounded terribly hollow and unconvincing.

"No doubt Mr. Clasby knows quite a bit about improper advances," Lord Grafton drawled.

Harriet felt the tension between the two men tighten to the breaking point, but she did not know what to do. Helpless, she watched Mr. Clasby stand. He looked so angry that she feared he might slap Lord Grafton right there and then.

"Miss Whitlow has honored me with her attentive ear," Mr. Clasby said with forced politeness. "An intelligent lady and a paragon of virtue, impropriety and Miss Whitlow could no more mix than oil and water." He then turned to her and bowed. "Your servant."

Lord Grafton did nothing but harrumph as he watched Mr. Clasby leave. Then he turned to her. "Why, Miss Whitlow, you have not touched your food."

"I have completely lost my appetite. Perhaps we might find my parents. I do believe I should like to leave."

Lord Grafton looked taken aback, but said nothing more on the matter. He offered Harriet his arm and they sought her parents.

Chapter Five

Lord Whitlow knew something was wrong. His daughter had spoken nary a word the short drive home, and if that were not proof enough, they had left Holland House early. He had just gone to the refreshment table for a second plate when Lord Grafton approached to ask if they might leave. Harriet would not even look at him.

Once home, she bid everyone a good night and headed up the stairs and into her room. His lady-wife soon followed after their daughter, leaving him alone with Lord Grafton, who looked hesitant to take his leave.

"Grafton," Lord Whitlow said, "would you care for a spot of brandy?"

"I should like that very much, sir."

"Come into my study then. It appears you have something on your mind." He slapped Grafton on the back and admired the breadth of the younger man's shoulders. He was a good-looking fellow and the perfect complement to his daughter's delicate beauty.

Once they were seated, with goblets half filled with amber-colored spirits in hand, Lord Whitlow asked, "So tell me, do you have any idea why my daughter should wish to depart early this evening?"

Grafton shifted in his seat. "I think it might have something to do with the impertinence of Mr. Clasby."

Lord Whitlow felt his ire rise quickly. He knew Clasby was a bounder! He would get to the bottom of it the next time he saw the rascal. But instead of making his opinion known, he merely raised his eyebrow and asked, "What makes you say so?"

"I came upon them, huddled close in discussion. I interrupted them, of course—" Grafton paused.

"Of course," Lord Whitlow agreed.

"Miss Whitlow appeared to be a trifle flustered, embarrassed, if you will. I think it had everything to do with what Clasby had said. An improper overture, no doubt."

"But you did not actually hear it." Lord Whitlow thought the man was showing signs of sensibilities that rivaled an elderly aunt, but then the boy might simply be jealous. Surely, that was a good sign.

"No, sir. But considering Clasby's past, one can only assume."

"I see. So you came to my daughter's rescue."

"I could not stand by and allow any insult leveled at Miss Whitlow."

Lord Whitlow digested this information as he swallowed a sip of brandy.

"As you know," Lord Grafton continued. "My desire is to offer for your daughter's hand."

"My boy," Lord Whitlow said, "you just have."

"'Pon rep, so you are right." He cleared his throat. "Might I have the honor of declaring myself and ask your permission to wed Miss Whitlow?"

Lord Whitlow knew Grafton's situation completely. He had recently inherited his sire's title, holdings, and wealth. Grafton had spelled out as much when he first asked permission to call. Lord Whitlow had done some checking on his own and he liked everything he saw and heard about the man. Grafton was neither a gambler nor did he indulge in the keeping of light skirts and ladybirds. He attended church services regularly and had even provided the funds for the renovation of the Grafton chapel once his father had passed.

Lord Whitlow wanted to accept this man who seemed perfect in every way for his Harriet, but something his wife once said gave him pause. *We know of him dear, but we do not really know him.*

"Grafton," Lord Whitlow said, "as much as I wish to make your way clear with my daughter, her happiness is what is most important to me. I give you my blessing and my permission to make your declaration to my daughter. But there will be no announcement, no understanding, if you will, until my daughter tells me that she wishes to accept you. You have some wooing to do, and I would not have it any other way."

Grafton bowed his head. "Thank you, Lord Whitlow." His brandy finished, he stood.

Lord Whitlow wished the lad well as he left, but remained troubled. Grafton did seem a bit pompous, even for an earl. He knew Harriet favored George Clasby. In fact, he believed that his wife held a soft spot for the scoundrel as well. She had reminded him often enough that Clasby was not so terribly different than he had been in his callow days of youth. And that's what worried him. Lord Whitlow knew too well the type of indiscretions Clasby had practiced. And he did not want that kind of history and experience to touch his innocent daughter.

The day of the Waterton-Smythes' garden party dawned with warm temperatures and sunny skies. The party started in the afternoon and would last well into the night. Chilled champagne and lemonade would be served along with watercress sandwiches and tea cakes until supper was announced. It would be held under tents followed by dancing into the wee hours.

Harriet dressed in a yellow muslin gown with long sleeves and a cone-shaped skirt with flounces starting nearly at the knee. The neckline had been brought down a little lower than before, but even so, Harriet grabbed a lace fichu and tucked it into the bodice. She could always remove it when she became overheated. She would definitely take it off before dancing.

When it was time to go, her mother gave her an encouraging nod as they climbed into their carriage. She had come to Harriet's room the night before, knowing her daughter was upset. Harriet had cautiously told her mother how Lord Grafton had insulted Mr. Clasby. Her mother had asked Harriet to give Grafton a chance, saying he was a good man whom her father held in high regard. Harriet had reluctantly agreed, but she knew in her heart Lord Grafton was not the man for her.

They pulled into the long drive of the large estate belonging to the Waterton-Smythes, which was mere blocks from their own town house, and waited in the line of carriages taking turns delivering various guests. Harriet leaned back, prepared to wait, since her parents, along with half the guest list, believed it more fashionable to arrive late than early. She wondered if Mr. Clasby was also in the carriage line.

Finally, after what seemed an eternity, they got out of the hot carriage and walked toward the rear gardens. Harriet needed something cool to drink. Without hesitation, she went straight to the refreshments tent. Her nerves were tense as she scanned the crowd for Lord Grafton. She was in no mood to withstand his hovering, even though she had promised to give the man the benefit of another chance.

She reached for a glass of iced lemonade and drank it in one gulp. She helped herself to a second glass and carried it with her as she moved into the lush gardens set up with archery lanes, a maypole complete with a tetherball, and an area cleared for battledore and shuttlecock.

Her lips curved into a broad smile when she spotted a dark red head of hair that shimmered with glints of gold. Mr. Clasby tested the rackets.

"Mr. Clasby," she said with a wave of her hand.

"Miss Whitlow." He bowed when she stood before him. "Good afternoon."

"A glorious day for a garden party." She had a terrible habit of stating the obvious when she first saw him, but such inane chatter helped calm her racing pulse.

"Indeed." He squinted into the sun. The fine lines around his eyes were noticeable and his hair ruffled in the warm breeze. He looked incredibly handsome. "I am in need of a partner. Would you care to join me?"

"I should like that above all things." She meant it with all her heart.

"Very well," he said. "I have challenged Lord and Lady Cherrington. In fact, we have just made a slight wager."

Harriet grinned as Artemis and her husband, Cherry, walked onto the area of play. With Mr. Clasby shining like the sun itself, she had not even noticed them. "Artie, how glad I am that you decided to come." Considering the mean-spirited comments the Waterton-Smythe sisters had made about Artemis last year during her come-out, Harriet thought she would have stayed away.

"I cannot keep my wife away from a party out-of-doors, you know," Lord Cherrington said as he whisked off his coat. "Good afternoon, Miss Whitlow."

"Lord Cherrington," Harriet said with a nod. "What are the terms of the wager?"

Artemis answered before her husband had the chance. "The losing team provides a picnic lunch for the winning team. I have already invited Mr. Clasby, and now I invite you, to join Cherry and I for a ride and picnic in the park tomorrow. Do say you will come." She waited for Harriet's answer.

Harriet could have hugged her friend. She offered a way to spend time with Mr. Clasby. "Of course I shall come. I would not dream of missing it, since I rather have a taste for meat pies. May the winning team choose the contents of the picnic basket?"

They laughed and then Mr. Clasby answered, "I do not see why not."

"Well then, Mr. Clasby, let us trounce them soundly." Harriet took the racket he offered.

"We have a very good chance to fulfill your desires, Miss Whitlow. I am quite an accomplished player."

"I am proficient but by no means do I excel," Harriet said. "Mr. Clasby, you shall have to help me."

"It will be my great pleasure to do so." He smiled at her, and Harriet thought she would melt into a puddle at his feet. He had a most charming smile.

They played for upwards of half of an hour,

their gentle taunts and laughter drawing a small crowd around them to watch. Finally Mr. Clasby scored the winning hit.

"Well done, Clasby," Artemis said.

"Indeed," Lord Cherrington agreed.

"I owe deep gratitude to my lovely partner for not allowing many to get past me." Mr. Clasby bowed and winked.

Harriet flushed with warmth under such an agreeable compliment. She had indeed played well even though she had missed a couple of shuttlecocks, giving points to their opponents when the feathered bits of cork hit the ground.

"I think we should make our way to the refreshments." Lord Cherrington offered his arm to his wife and they left, leaving Harriet and Mr. Clasby behind to gather up the shuttlecocks.

"That was most fun," Harriet said.

"I thought so," Mr. Clasby agreed.

Harriet handed him her battledore racket just as Lord Grafton approached.

"Perhaps we might offer a challenge," Lord Grafton said seriously.

The younger Miss Waterton-Smythe hung upon Lord Grafton's arm and smirked as if partnering him was the accomplishment of the Season.

"Perhaps Miss Whitlow is tired," Mr. Clasby said.

Harriet was not about to refuse another half of an hour in Mr. Clasby's presence. Tired or no, she would play in the hope of beating their opponents. "I can go another round."

"Very well, shall we play until the first team reaches fifteen points?" Lord Grafton slid off his coat and draped it across a chair.

"That is the usual number needed," Mr. Clasby said.

"Indeed, for gentlemen, but with the weaker sex, perhaps they would rather play only to eleven," Lord Grafton explained.

"Fifteen is fine, my lord," Harriet said quickly. She did not care to be referred to as weak. A servant carried a tray of refreshments toward them, and Harriet knew that Artemis must have ordered their delivery. Glasses of lemonade were placed neatly beside elegant crystal goblets of champagne that sparkled in the sunshine.

Harriet did not quite know why she chose the champagne. Later, she would congratulate herself on the genius of it. But for now, the champagne looked incredibly refreshing compared to plain lemonade and she longed to taste its cool sweetness. She downed her glass and helped herself to another when she noticed that Lord Grafton's eyebrow rose up with obvious displeasure.

Perhaps it was the heady feeling of having won the last match that had emboldened her, or perhaps it was the friendly teasing that she and Mr. Clasby had engaged in with Artie and Lord Cherrington earlier. Whatever it was, Harriet felt a little naughty. She wanted to give Lord Grafton of bit of his own rude medicine.

Instead of behaving as she should, she raised her second glass toward Lord Grafton with a cocksure nod and a toast. "May the best team win!

And that team will be Mr. Clasby and I," she said.

Mr. Clasby handed her the battledore as he took her empty glass and gave it to the footman. "You are taunting our opponents, Miss Whitlow," he whispered for her ears alone. "And I quite like it."

"Then let us come out on top, and it shall simply be a statement of fact."

"Miss Whitlow, I like the way you think."

"Let us hope you like the way I play, Mr. Clasby." Harriet took her place and wobbled. Her head spun and she had to blink her eyes a couple of times. Oh dear! Mayhap she should not have drunk the champagne. She was not used to its effects. The only spirits she had ever imbibed were mulled or sweet wines during the holidays.

Miss Waterton-Smythe served with surprising accuracy, but Harriet's legs felt bolted to the ground. It was difficult to move them yet she did so slowly. She swung and missed the shuttlecock.

Mr. Clasby, ever a fine example of athletics, came up behind her and sent the thing sailing high into the air toward Lord Grafton.

Lord Grafton returned the volley with more vigor than needed. The shuttlecock dove toward the ground but Mr. Clasby was able to return it with a flourish, causing Lord Grafton to miss. The shuttlecock fell to the ground.

"Our point," Mr. Clasby announced.

Harriet turned to smile, and that quick action made her see stars. She focused on her partner as he served the shuttlecock. Lord Grafton rallied and volleyed it back. Harriet ran to return it and she collided with Mr. Clasby.

She lost her balance and fell, but strong arms quickly grasped her waist bringing her in direct contact with a solid chest. Then her foot tangled with his and Mr. Clasby fell backwards, taking her with him. They landed with a thud on the soft grass.

George took a deep breath, filling his lungs with air that had been momentarily knocked out of him. His arms tightened around the slender armful that was Miss Whitlow. He tipped his head up and looked into her laughing eyes. They were quite sprawled together in a heap.

Miss Whitlow looked at him and the merriment changed to an awkward awareness. She blushed furiously and did not know where to look. And then her helpless gaze returned to his and she licked her lips. George felt a shudder of warmth pump through him. He knew he had better move quickly before he did something he'd soon regret.

"Miss Whitlow," he said. "Might you get up?"

She grimaced as she moved. "I do not think I can," she said.

George looked past Harriet, straight into Lord Grafton's serious stare bearing down on him.

"Is something wrong?" Lord Grafton drawled.

George laughed out loud. Of course something was wrong! Harriet Whitlow was draped across him like a bedsheet and he liked the feel of it far more than he should. If something was not done fast, Miss Whitlow would soon understand just how much he enjoyed their position. "Could you lend Miss Whitlow a hand?" George asked.

Lord Grafton bent down to give her aid, and George rolled out from under her and stood up. Miss Whitlow remained on her knees.

"Oh dear!" Her face twisted with pain when she tried to stand.

"What is it?" George asked. "What hurts?"

"My foot," she groaned.

"Do not say that I stepped upon it. Grafton"—George pointed—"grab her elbow, will you? I'll do the same on this side and let us lift her up gently on the count of three. One . . . two . . . three."

She stood but groaned when she put her full weight upon her foot. George swept her up into his arms and carried her off the field. Several onlookers stopped to look, cluck, or *tsk* before moving on.

"Should I fetch your mother?" Miss Waterton-Smythe asked. She held onto Lord Grafton's arm as if she were faint.

George actually pitied Grafton, who was trying to disengage from her grasp.

"No!" Miss Whitlow nearly shouted, then added more softly, "That is to say, I think I shall be right as rain if I could rest a moment."

"Grafton, fetch that chair there, will you?" George gestured with a nod of his head. "Let's get Miss Whitlow out of the sun."

"Very well, Clasby, and something cold to drink would no doubt be beneficial. Lemonade this time," Grafton said sternly.

George gently lowered Miss Whitlow into the chair and then knelt down by her feet.

"And ice, if you can manage it," George called out to the back of the departing lord. Miss Waterton-Smythe, not one to be left behind and forgotten by an eligible peer with exceptionally warm pockets, scampered after him with promises to help.

"I suppose we must forfeit our game and I shall have to eat my words." Miss Whitlow pulled the scrap of lace out from her bodice. He saw the sheen of perspiration that had gathered in the center of her chest glisten. Fascinated, he watched a bead of sweat trickle down her skin to disappear into creamy cleavage.

He quickly looked into her eyes, ashamed. "Might I have a look at your, uh, foot?"

She blushed even deeper and raised the hem of her skirt. "Of course, but surely it is not broken. Most likely only bruised."

"Better to be certain." He reached toward a very delicately turned ankle and hesitated. He felt a sticky bit of his own sweat run down his back.

"I won't bite," she said with a low giggle. It did not help matters.

"No, but your father might," George muttered. He would be better off if the Waterton-Smythe chit searched out Lady Whitlow after all. He did not wish to be accused of any improprieties.

"Oh, pish and fiddle," Miss Whitlow said. "I have had an accident. You are merely acting in a medical capacity. What harm can there be?"

The situation could be plenty harmful, George

thought, but he pushed the idea aside. They were away from prying eyes, considering that they sat beneath a towering hedgerow, but it could hardly be construed as a compromising location. Even so, he cautiously felt from her ankle to the tips of her toes as if he were touching a delicate sugar loaf that might crumble once his fingers made contact. And he properly turned his head away.

"George, do not be so missish," she said with another giggle.

He looked up sharply. He liked the way his name sounded in her sultry voice. But she seemed almost silly. Surely she was not foxed on two glasses of champagne.

"Might I call you George?" she asked, suddenly shy.

"Of course you may."

"And you must call me Harriet." She smiled.

"Very well, Harriet. Wiggle your toes."

She did as he had instructed, stifling yet another giggle.

"Nothing appears to be broken," he said.

"Here." Grafton returned and set a small bucket filled with chipped ice upon the ground. He handed a glass of lemonade to Harriet.

She smiled politely and accepted it for a deep sip. Her merry gaze connected with George's over the rim of the glass. There was definite mischief in her gray orbs and he was never so relieved to have the pompous Lord Grafton at his side.

"Might I use your lace scarf?" George asked. "There is a definite bruise developing and it looks puffy."

Harriet handed it to him, and he filled a section with the ice that Grafton had brought. "Grafton, might you help me tie this?" George asked. He had to keep his thoughts focused on the task at hand. Harriet's bold looks were too much of a temptation.

Grafton bent down on his knee, and the two of them fashioned an icy splint of sorts and tied it about Harriet's foot. It was awkward and Grafton looked completely uncomfortable, as if he had never touched a woman before.

"Miss Waterton-Smythe has gone to fetch your mother, Miss Whitlow. They shall be here momentarily," Grafton said.

"Thank you, my lord." Harriet's voice sounded dull and just slightly disappointed.

The minx, George thought. She enjoyed the attention of two men fussing over her, as any lady would. Lord Grafton looked decidedly disagreeable about the whole affair. George knew the uptight earl was wishing him to Hades, but even so, George was deuced glad Grafton was there.

George remembered too well how nice Harriet had felt in his arms. She had melted into him much the same way at Rothwell Park under the mistletoe. George had cast aside all thoughts of that kiss as merely the effects of mulled wine and the joyous spirit of the holiday. And now Miss Whitlow had imbibed once again.

It would be relatively easy to take advantage of her tipsy state. He was tempted to experience another kiss, just to see if she would respond with such sweet surrender yet again. He dared not, else he'd bring the wrath of her father down around his ears.

"Miss Whitlow," George said. "I leave you in capable hands, and your mother is coming even now."

"But Mr. Clasby," Harriet said quickly.

"Yes?"

"The picnic."

"Ah yes, I will send a footman round tomorrow to see how you feel. If your foot still troubles you, I will bring my curricle."

"Thank you, Mr. Clasby. I shall inform Lord and Lady Cherrington."

"Miss Whitlow, do rest and heed your mother's words. I shall seek out the Cherringtons this very minute." He bowed and took his leave without another glance backwards. He tried to shake the dizzying feel of Harriet Whitlow pressed close against him. She felt too nice in his arms for comfort. Much too nice.

Chapter Six

*H*arriet sat at the table in the breakfast room with her foot resting upon a pillow as her father perused the *Morning Post* and her mother refilled her chocolate. No one spoke. But Harriet anxiously wondered how she should phrase her request to go on the picnic as planned. She wanted assurance of a positive response.

She nibbled her toast and fretted over how to broach the subject. Her parents had grudgingly given their permission the day before on the grounds that her foot must improve. The tiny bit of swelling had gone down completely, leaving behind an ugly bruise. She could walk but still experienced a painful twinge when she put her full weight upon it. She dared not admit it, or she would have no chance of going anywhere.

It was deplorable to have missed the dancing under the tents the previous evening. Concerned over her foot, her parents brought her home early and sent her straight to bed to rest. She had never slept so long in her life!

She sipped her chocolate, hoping for an opportune moment to voice her request. It would be far worse to stay home today. She breathed deep for courage and opened her mouth to broach the subject weighing heavily on her mind, when the butler announced Mr. Clasby's arrival.

"Shall I send him back, my lord?" the butler asked.

Harriet glanced quickly at her father, who looked surprised and not a little annoyed to have his breakfast interrupted. When he hesitated to respond, Harriet closed her eyes. Surely he would not turn Mr. Clasby away.

"Show him in," her father finally answered.

Harriet let out the breath she had been holding.

After a few moments, Mr. Clasby stepped through the doorway. His thick auburn hair had been carefully combed off his forehead. In his eyes, she read the wariness he must feel. George looked a little intimidated by her father, which Harriet found endearing.

"Good morning," Mr. Clasby said with a bow. "I apologize for my early call. I was in the area and wished to check on Miss Whitlow's injury caused by my own wretched clumsiness, I am afraid."

"How good of you to inquire in person," her mother said with a soft smile. "Accidents do happen."

George looked relieved. "Indeed they do. And

because they do, I did not wish to assume that Miss Whitlow was feeling up to our picnic this afternoon with Lord and Lady Cherrington." He stood with his hands behind his back and waited.

Harriet's gaze darted to her father, and her heart pounded with hope.

"Mr. Clasby, I appreciate your concern. I believe a carriage is a must since Harriet is still limping." Her father turned toward her. "Are you up to an outing?"

"I am," Harriet squeaked out. She could manage to ride sidesaddle, but sitting beside George in his open carriage would be much more agreeable.

"Very well." Mr. Clasby bowed. "I shall return with my curricle at three o'clock to collect Miss Whitlow."

Her father rose to his feet. "I shall walk you out."

Harriet glanced quickly at Mr. Clasby, who did not appear the least bit comfortable as he followed her father out of the room.

"What was that about?" Harriet asked her mother.

"I do not know, dear."

George pulled at his cravat. He did not much care for the irritated gleam in Whitlow's eye, but he obediently followed the gentleman into his study. His nerves tightened further when Lord Whitlow closed the door. "Is there something amiss, my lord?"

"Mr. Clasby." Whitlow gestured for him to sit down. He took his place behind a huge desk. "It has come to my attention that your conversation has made my daughter uncomfortable."

Confused and not a little nervous, George looked Harriet's father directly in the eye. "I must humbly beg your pardon and that of your daughter. If Miss Whitlow wishes to forgo my company, I will cease calling. Just say the word."

Whitlow raised his hand. "Now just hold on. Perhaps I have said it all wrong. Harriet has stated nothing of the kind. She claims that you are her friend, after all. 'Tis simply that I heard one version and I would like to hear your side of it."

George was even more confused. "Begging your pardon, but I do not quite follow you."

"Let me be direct then." He leaned forward. "At the literary evening at Holland House, did you speak about an inappropriate subject which may have caused Miss Whitlow distress?"

George felt himself flush. Water closets and bathing fixtures were not exactly casual conversation, but he did not think the topic had bothered Harriet in the least.

Whitlow leaned back satisfied, wearing his usual know-it-all expression. "I see your old ways have not completely escaped you. Your lack of discretion has been found out and I believe your association with my daughter must come to an end."

George jumped to his feet. "It is not as you imagine, my lord."

Whitlow also stood. "Then it is true, you have played fast and loose with my daughter? I have warned you—"

"I have done no such thing," George sputtered with offense. "True, I did broach a topic not common for polite conversation, but it had everything to do with the improvements I have been making to the *necessary* at my estate and nothing to do with—well, that goes without saying." George felt the heat in his ears and knew his face must be red also.

"You have made no improper advances?" Lord Whitlow looked almost disappointed.

"Upon my word, I have not." In his thoughts he had, perhaps, but he was not about to admit *that* to the girl's father. Then he remembered that Lord Grafton had uttered that exact phrase. Improper advances, indeed. Grafton had tattled where nothing needed be told!

"My lord," George started. "I give you my word as a gentleman that I have no intention of leading your daughter astray. If she wishes Lord Grafton's affection, I will not stand in the way."

"If only it were that simple," Lord Whitlow muttered.

"How's that, sir?"

"Nothing. Nothing at all. I thank you, Mr. Clasby, for obliging an overly protective parent."

George bowed. He had effectively been dismissed with out so much as an apology. "I can show myself out, my lord."

"Very well."

George took his leave, but he could not help but wonder what the devil Grafton was up to telling Whitlow such taradiddles. Lord Whitlow had not look pleased with George's innocence, either. It was almost as if the man had wished George was playing the seducer with Harriet.

Botheration! Was it possible that Miss Whitlow was not interested in the lofty paragon of virtue that was Lord Grafton? But even if that were so, it did not change the fact that he had just promised not to interfere with their courtship. George left the Whitlow town house with worry gnawing at his thoughts.

He had stumbled into a family drama more troublesome than he had bargained for. He teetered too close to respectability to ruin it all now. If he ruined Harriet's chances with Grafton, whether perceived or not, George did not want the responsibility of Harriet's choice laid at his feet. Underneath Whitlow's polite exterior, George knew the man was looking for the slightest reason to send him packing permanently. And that was indeed disappointing.

Harriet peeked through the lace curtains and watched as George expertly pulled his curricle to the curb. She experienced the familiar racing of her heart that always accompanied the mere sight of him.

"Is Mr. Clasby here?" her mother asked without looking up from her needlepoint.

"He is." Harriet stood and put on her pelisse. The day had remained warm but the breeze was cool.

"Have a lovely time, dear. And do be careful of your foot."

"Of course, Mama, I promise that I will," Harriet said just as their butler announced Mr. Clasby.

"Lady Whitlow," George bowed. "Miss Whitlow, are you ready? Lord and Lady Cherrington are waiting outside."

"I am." Harriet took his offered arm. She experienced a shiver down her spine when his gloved hand covered her own and squeezed.

"If you become tired, say the word, and I shall bring you back immediately," George said softly.

"I am not quite right as rain, but close enough. A picnic poses no threat to my health, I assure you."

"Even so." George bowed his head to the butler who opened the door wide for them.

Artemis and Cherry were perched on their mounts, no doubt planning to ride later. That suited Harriet very well since she would have George all to herself. She smiled broadly at Artemis. Harriet was grateful to her friend for providing an opportunity to spend time with Mr. Clasby unhindered by other callers, especially Lord Grafton.

Cherry gave Harriet an encouraging nod, and she knew that Artemis had told her husband about the *tendre* she had nursed for Mr. Clasby over the years. Harriet did not mind. In fact she was glad that she had not read pity or disapproval in Lord Cherrington's eyes. He appeared to understand her situation.

"Here, let me help you." George lifted her up into the seat.

She was breathless when he jumped up next to her. She inhaled deeply of the woodsy cologne he wore mixed with the scent of soap. She wanted to slide a little closer to him, but instead, she sat frozen in place.

With a click of the reins they were on their way, but Harriet remained quiet. She suffered from a sudden case of nerves. She feared that whatever she might say would sound ridiculous and so she remained quiet the short distance into Hyde Park, silently berating herself as the worst sort of coward the whole way.

When they made their way to a secluded corner of the park, they laid their blankets and baskets under a huge oak tree with a massive spread of branches. Harriet pulled her pelisse more closely about her shoulders to ward off the slight chill in the air. The men tended to the horses and she helped Artemis empty the vast amount of food from the basket.

"I had Cook prepare the meat pies you requested, Harriet." Artemis lifted a large tin.

"I can hardly wait to try one," Harriet said. "We often eat them in the country, but once in town, Father thinks they are too provincial and not in character with our lofty station."

Artemis laughed at Harriet's imitation of her father. "How are things progressing with Mr. Clasby?" she whispered quickly.

"I do not know," Harriet whispered back. "Lord Grafton often ruins everything by chasing George away."

"I see." Artemis snitched a piece of cheese and popped it into her mouth. "Perhaps you need to be more direct with Mr. Clasby. Does he have any idea where your preferences lay?"

"Again, I do not know." Harriet chewed her bottom lip. "I cannot seem to form the words to tell him."

"Sometimes words are not needed, my dear," Artemis said with a wink.

Harriet wanted to discuss the matter further, but the men had finished securing the horses and sat down, promptly ending the discussion. Harriet knew Artemis was correct—she had given George no hint of her true feelings. But how did one go about doing such a thing? She was not accustomed to expressing her wants and desires, especially when they went against her parents' wishes.

"Mr. Clasby," she said, offering him a plate. "Do you like meat pies?" Her stomach felt weak. She had to let him know that she welcomed his advances.

Lord Grafton's accusation that Mr. Clasby was well versed with improper advances rang in her ears and she furiously pushed it aside. Mr. Clasby had been nothing but proper toward her and that was what truly mattered.

A very improper image of the two of them trying out his bathing invention suddenly flashed through her mind. Her cheeks grew warm and she could hardly look at him without imagining him without his shirt and waistcoat. Would his chest be bare and smooth like her brother's or would there be a mat of hair?

She had come upon her brother and his friends swimming a few summers ago only to have them tease her by threatening to come out of the water and chase her. She dashed back home in a trice, but had received an eyeful of nearly naked young men.

"I thought you were going to call me George." He smiled as he took an offered pie.

"Forgive me, George," she answered with a flustered shrug of her shoulders. She quickly dug through the basket for a napkin.

"I do have quite an appetite for meat pies," George said. "One of the things I love about London is that they are sold nearly everywhere."

Lord Cherrington produced glasses and a bottle. "I brought wine."

"And fruit and cheese and raspberry tartlets," Artemis added.

"A veritable feast," George said before taking a hearty bite into his meat pie.

The meal progressed with the conversation centered upon their match of battledore and shuttlecock, which inevitably led to the telling of how Harriet managed to trip into George and land in a heap.

"See, 'tis still bruised." Harriet flexed her foot, covered by silken hose and a loosely laced slipper.

"I must have stepped upon it before we fell," George said. "I am heartily sorry for it."

"I hardly think it your error. We were both chasing the same shuttlecock when you trod upon my poor foot," Harriet said. "I think the error was mine alone in that I drank two glasses of champagne far too quickly. I am unused to spirits."

"I say! And here we are plying Miss Whitlow

with wine." Lord Cherrington helped himself to a tartlet. "Watch out Clasby, else she run into you again."

"Then I shall simply have to catch her—again."

Harriet looked into George's copper-colored eyes, which were filled with merriment, and she was momentarily lost. He teased her, she knew, but she wondered if he too wanted to experience the sensation of being locked in each other's arms all over again. She had been ill prepared for it yesterday and unable to respond in a manner other than confusion and embarrassment.

A flirtatious comment dangled on the tip of her tongue only to falter into oblivion. She wanted to tell him that she would enjoy being caught, but the words shriveled and died before they could be uttered. Oh, but she was a horrible flirt! At this rate she would end up an old spinster before she worked up the courage to express her affection.

"Well, Cherry." Artemis stood and shook out the skirts of her riding habit. "Shall we ride?"

"Indeed, madam-wife." Lord Cherrington turned to face Harriet. "Do you mind, my dear?"

"Not in the least." Harriet turned to George. "As long as Mr. Clasby does not mind keeping me company."

"It would be my pleasure."

"Very well. We shan't be long." Lord Cherrington followed Artemis to the horses and in moments they were gone.

Harriet had been looking forward to a moment alone with George for days. But now that she was faced with her desire, she felt terribly self-conscious. She glanced at George as he fiddled with his napkin, folding and unfolding it.

"Would you care for anything more to eat?" she asked.

George placed his hand on his stomach. "I could not touch another morsel." He stood up and extended his hand. "Would you like to walk? That is, if your foot does not trouble you too much."

"That would be very nice." Harriet took his hand, stood, and then looped her arm through his.

"You will tell me if you need to go back?"

"Of course."

"I am dreadfully sorry for hurting you," George said. His hand rested upon her bare forearm and she relished the feel of his skin touching hers.

"Like I said earlier, it was not your fault. Simply an accident."

"I think we would have beaten Grafton and Miss Waterton-Smythe had we played a full game."

"I would have thoroughly enjoyed trouncing them," Harriet said with relish.

"To show off your skill for Lord Grafton?" George asked.

Harriet stumbled but George steadied her by pulling her close. She looked up into his eyes and knew it was now or never. "My father is the one who appreciates Lord Grafton's charms."

George's eyes clouded over with an expression Harriet could not identify. "By all accounts, he is a good man," he said with a hollow voice. "He would no doubt make you a fine husband."

Harriet was not sure why George would sing

Lord Grafton's praises; the two men had rubbed each other the wrong way since meeting. Was this his way of letting her know that he was not interested in her? A cutting pain sliced through her chest. He had only called upon her to help restore his name in the eyes of the *ton*.

His image had improved and he received several good invitations. Did he feel he had accomplished his aim and did not need her any longer? Or was she so insufferably dull that George had decided he wanted nothing more to do with her? Her eyes burned suspiciously and she feared tears were not far from the surface.

"Mr. Clasby," she managed to say around the lump in her throat. "Perhaps I cannot walk as far as I thought."

George sat in his club, a cheroot smoldering between his lips and a half empty glass of brandy in his hand. *What a fine kettle of fish*, he thought. He wanted to call on Harriet Whitlow in earnest, yet he had promised her father he would not come between her and Lord Grafton. *The devil take it!*

He exhaled a long tendril of smoke and muttered another oath. Harriet was not exactly what he wanted in a woman, but there was something about her that drew him. He had always hoped to be struck by love at first sight so that his decision would be instant, with little need for logic or extensive considerations.

He didn't love Harriet. She was sweet as could be, and he felt genuine desire when he held her, but was that enough to risk the wrath of her father? He doubted it. Her father would never approve the match, so he was wasting his time even thinking about it.

He should have known this would happen after that blasted kiss at Christmas! She kissed like an angel and had the voice of a temptress, but she was an innocent and religious to boot. He had never wanted much to do with the church. Perhaps losing both parents at a young age tended to harden one's heart toward God and heavenly matters.

Regardless, Grafton was the favored man. But he was an arrogant, high in the instep lobcock who made a poor match for a lady of such generosity. Miss Whitlow had never let her high social standing get in the way of showing kindness to one and all.

Especially him. She had always treated him with respect instead of looking down her nose as if he were a speck of dirt on the carpet or worse. And never did she appear fascinated by the gossip of his paramours.

"What's got you looking so glum?" Jory DeVillars asked.

"Nothing," George grunted.

"My sister says your name is seeing less tarnish and your invitations are multiplying." DeVillars pulled out a chair. "I have also heard your name linked most often with that of Miss Whitlow. Confound it man, you have turned over a broad new leaf."

George sat up straight at the mention of Harriet. "Just what have you heard?" He leaned closer to DeVillars.

"Easy now," DeVillars said. "Nothing bad."

"Then what?" George persisted.

"Only that you'll never have a chance to offer for Miss Whitlow. Grafton's as good as got Whitlow's permission. He has only to ask the lady in question. He will quite beat you to it, you know."

"I have no intention of offering for Miss Whitlow." George leaned back in his seat and took another puff of his cheroot.

"Why not?"

George hesitated. He had not told anyone other than Whitlow that he wanted to call on Harriet only to save his reputation. It seemed as nothing before, but now—he felt ashamed. "Like you have said, she can do far better than me."

"That goes with out saying." DeVillars laughed. "But there are those who disagree. In fact, some of us have placed a wager upon it."

Anger pumped through George's veins until he narrowed his eyes to mere slits. "I do not care to have Miss Whitlow the subject of wagers around Boodle's taproom, if you please."

"Too late, it's done. Check the books. The wager is there."

"Blast your eyes, DeVillars!" George stood to his feet. "Is this your doing?"

"Come now, Clasby, sit back down," DeVillars said calmly. "You are the one who started this charade in the first place. Paying your addresses to an innocent, leaving off from any indecent contact with women, including the demi-monde."

"I've never been fond of light-skirts and you know it." George sat down.

" 'Course not, and why should you? You've always been the kept one, have you not? A plaything for lonely women of wealth in society. But now it seems that you have chosen a different path and we're cheering you on, Clasby. Truly we are. You appear willing to place your head in the noose of matrimony, but why did you set your sights so high as the lofty Miss Whitlow? My reputation is not nearly as bad and her father put a bug in my ear her first Season. Whatever were you thinking?"

"You have all been discussing this, have you? Entertaining, I am sure," George grumbled.

DeVillars laughed again. "Care about her, do you? More's the pity. Make your life miserable that way."

George shook his head. "She is merely a dear friend."

That admission made DeVillars laugh even harder. "Was it not you who informed us all that men and women can never be friends?"

George flushed slightly. It was true. He had viewed women through narrow windows most of his life. Never had he called a woman *friend*; not until he had met Harriet.

She had been so fearful her first Season. George remembered clearly how she had hung back, not pushing herself forward as the other young ladies making their bows had. But she had smiled shyly at him when he had teased her. Laughed when he told a joke. He had always thought her pretty, but not his type. Harriet Whitlow's looks were soft and gentle. A man could ease his troubled soul just by contemplating her delicate beauty.

By the following Season, she had more town bronze that she used to easily slip in and around the best society had to offer. Respect for her increased as did the long line of gentlemen vying for her hand. But Whitlow always managed to whittle that list down to only one or two. Even so, Harriet had remained unwed.

Later that year, he saw her at the Rothwells' hunting party. Harriet was a stable presence in an otherwise mad scavenger hunt to capture Lord Ashbourne's attention. She had befriended Rothwell's daughter, Artemis, when the other ladies shunned her because of her hoydenish behavior.

It was not difficult to like Harriet Whitlow. In fact, after calling upon this Season's Incomparables and other notable young ladies making their first and even second bows to society, George's good opinion of Miss Whitlow had only increased. Not one lady made him feel as comfortable as had Harriet.

George had never entertained thoughts of desire for her—until now. She had always seemed like a friend's little sister. One did not seek warmer feelings from a friend, but against his better judgment, George suddenly wished to do just that.

Chapter Seven

"*W*hat is it, dear?" his wife looked at him through her vanity mirror.

"That dashed Clasby fellow appears to be on the level," Lord Whitlow fumed. It was his wife's doing that he gave the rascal permission to call upon Harriet. And now the blasted man was well on his way to proving himself!

"Whatever do you mean?"

"That night at Holland House, Lord Grafton told me that Clasby had upset Harriet by making improper advances. I confronted Clasby on the matter. He informed me that the only impropriety was the subject of their discussion. I understand Mr. Clasby likes to tinker with his indoor plumbing."

His wife laughed softly, showing no regard for the seriousness of the matter. "Is that why you followed him out this morning?" She did not wait for him to answer. "I already knew that."

"How did you know?" He stood behind his wife and helped her unclasp the heavy ruby necklace she wore.

"Harriet told me as much. In fact, she was quite incensed with Lord Grafton's behavior. He insulted poor Mr. Clasby."

"Why did you not tell me?"

"Because, dear," his wife said calmly. "Some things a man must discover on his own."

"Harumph," Lord Whitlow replied.

"Besides, you would have only accused me of placing myself on Mr. Clasby's side."

"A place you have firmly been for ever and a day, my love."

"Beneath Mr. Clasby's charming and rakish façade, I see a man of character," his wife told him. "He has lost his way, but I believe our Harriet will help him find his true path."

"Come now, what if your Mr. Clasby leads Harriet astray, or worse, returns to his paramours and breaks our little girl's heart in the process?" He shook his head. "No, no, she is much better off with Grafton. He is the safer man."

His wife turned in her chair to face him. "You cannot protect Harriet forever. She is a grown woman. Perhaps 'tis time we let our little one out from the safety of her parents' wings. It is past time she flew on her own, my dear. Trust her, Farley. She is a smart girl who knows her own heart, but she will not for the world let you down. You must tell your daughter that you will support her choice. If Mr. Clasby proves to be true, then let it be."

"I have given her more freedoms, just as you have suggested. Did I not act with complete restraint when she lowered her necklines?"

"Yes, you behaved admirably. But you must accept the fact that Harriet is an adult now."

Lord Whitlow knew his wife's words were true but he did not wish to believe them. Images of Harriet as a small girl flashed before his eyes. She was ever a tentative child, never straying far or getting into mischief. Harriet was nothing like Frederick, their eldest, who pulled away from his parents' leading strings since he could walk. His son had always vexed him with his unabashed independence and strong sense of pride, but Whitlow eventually grew to appreciate those very same qualities.

Harriet had always been his "little mite." He had been in the habit of protecting her very early as he urged her to take her first steps out of his shielding arms. He had also wiped the little tears that were shed whenever she had fallen.

Tears from his daughter managed to rent his heart since she seldom cried. She had always been a brave little soul, holding in any hurts or even her anger. He made a habit of doing everything in his power to keep unpleasantness from ever touching Harriet. After twenty-one years of practice, it was difficult to cut the invisible leading strings that Whitlow had carefully cultivated.

He held out his hands to his wife to help her rise from her vanity and come to bed. "You are no doubt correct, madam-wife, but do give me more time to consider these gentlemen. I am not convinced of Mr. Clasby's character as of yet. Until I am, I cannot in good conscience give my blessing."

*   *   *

Harriet, with the company of her maid, Sally, met Artemis early the next morning at her mantuamaker's shop on Bond Street. Harriet had several more gowns made over; plus, she needed to look at costume possibilities for the upcoming masquerade Lord and Lady Ponsonby held every year. Artemis and Cherry planned to attend dressed as Greek gods.

While they drank tea and nibbled biscuits, Harriet thumbed through catalogs of costumes.

"You are unusually quiet this morning," Artemis said.

"I beg your pardon, Artie, for my dour mood."

"What is wrong?"

"I do not think Mr. Clasby has any interest in me." Harriet had been dwelling on what had transpired between them on the picnic all morning.

"Harriet, do not dare say you are giving up. What happened?" Artemis refilled their dishes with tea.

"He thinks Lord Grafton a good match for me!"

"Of course he does. He and half the *ton* think so because it is quite known that your father supports the match."

Harriet chewed her bottom lip. It was so much easier to worship George Clasby from afar. Since he had started calling on her, their easy manner with each other was disintegrating into awkwardness and stretches of silence as if neither knew what to say to the other. It was most disheartening to find George at a loss for words. She had always relied on him to carry their conversations.

"If you want my opinion," Artemis said between nibbles of a biscuit. "I think Clasby cares for you but does not quite know what to do about it."

"What are you saying?" A bud of renewed hope sprang to life inside Harriet's heart.

"Did you notice how he looked at you yesterday? Like he was contemplating forbidden fruit."

Harriet laughed out loud. She had never been compared to the *forbidden* before. "Are you serious?"

"Quite."

Harriet gave a shadow of a smile to her friend. "I do not know. He seemed uncomfortable when we were alone."

"Exactly my point," Artemis said. "Harriet, you said he called on you simply to improve his reputation, and you were grateful for the chance to enslave him with your charms. Now stop. Do not make a face. What if you are succeeding, much to Clasby's surprise?"

"Do you really think so?"

"What other explanation can there be?"

"He thinks I am completely dull?" Harriet squeaked.

"But you are not. You cannot be, for if you were, he would no doubt have taken Lady Ellerton up on her offer."

"What?"

"Cherry heard at Boodle's that Clasby declined the invitations of Lady Ellerton."

"Truly?"

"If Clasby were not serious about changing his ways, or if you bored him in any way, surely he would have taken up with her on the sly. Do you not think?"

"Honestly, Artie," Harriet said with a sigh. "I just do not know."

Artemis waved her hand in dismissal of Harriet's doubts. "Now then, back to the business at hand. What costume will you choose to seduce him with at the Ponsonbys' party next week?"

"Artie!" Harriet gasped but then she sank into a fit of giggles, relieved and revived by Artemis' encouragement. *Seduce Mr. Clasby*, Harriet thought. *As if I would ever do such a thing!*

After discussing several possibilities, Harriet promised Artemis she would let her know her choice as soon as it was made. They left the shop and parted ways, since Harriet had some books to return to the bookseller shop she frequented.

After depositing the packages in the carriage, Harriet and Sally walked the short block to the small bookstore that catered to many of the ladies of the *ton* by allowing the leasing of books for a mere three pence. Harriet had in turn bought many of the books that she had borrowed. She opened the door and a tiny bell rang, announcing a customer.

"Good morning, Miss Whitlow," the clerk said with a bow.

"Good morning, Mr. Smith. How is your dear wife?"

"Fine indeed. I will tell her you asked."

"She makes the very best dish of tea," Harriet whispered. "Tell her I said so."

"She'll be tickled to hear." Mr. Smith beamed with pride.

"I would like to return these." Harriet set the

books on the counter. "And do you have any copies of Scott's *Ivanhoe*?"

"Indeed I did, Miss. I have just sold the last one to a gentleman only a moment ago," Mr. Smith said. "But we will be getting more. I can hold one for you."

"Yes, please do." Harriet decided that she must purchase a copy for George as a gift. It would be a start in her campaign to court him.

She turned to leave when she noticed that George stood in between two bookshelves, the novel *Ivanhoe* in his hand. "Mr. Clasby," she breathed. Her heart did its usual dance and flutters.

He looked up as if just noticing that others were in the shop. "Miss Whitlow, what a pleasant surprise." His smile was warm and genuine.

"You purchased a novel by Scott? I thought you found him dull."

"Since you adore the author so, I thought I should at least give the man a go." He held up his purchase. "I have already read the first two pages."

Harriet drew closer. "Do you like it? That is my favorite book, you know." She tried to see where he had left off from reading.

"Indeed, I do." George said. "Would you care to discuss the matter further over an ice at Gunter's? Perhaps we might read the first chapter together."

Warmth spread through Harriet like hot tea. "Yes. Let us go at once."

"Very well." He offered his arm after relieving

Sally of a small package Harriet had purchased on the way to the bookseller's.

Gunter's was not far, but even so, the three of them climbed into the crested Whitlow carriage. George seated himself very properly across from her, his back facing traffic. Harriet rode the whole way desperately trying not to stare at him. She wondered if what Artemis had said was true. Was there yet hope that George might one day fall in love with her? She had prayed for so long that it was difficult to remain confident in the dear Lord answering her pleas.

In no time they were seated at a table, two ices in hand. Harriet's maid wished to run some errands of her own and promised to return in an hour.

"Mr. Clasby, do you attend the Ponsonby masquerade?" she asked as she swished her lemon ice around in her cup.

His copper eyes shone with merriment. "I was most pleased to receive an invitation, unlike last year. Yes, Miss Whitlow, I will certainly be there."

"Have you decided upon a costume?"

"I have not. Have you?"

Harriet took another bite of lemon ice. "I have considered several possibilities, but I have not decided."

"Care to share those choices?"

Harriet smiled. "Of course. Perhaps you might help me make my decision. Boudicea the warrior queen—"

George made a face. "Goodness, Harriet, you

are far too gentle for such a costume. You would hardly look the part."

Harriet scrunched her nose. "I suppose you are correct. I could always dress as a fairy or a princess, perhaps."

"You are far more suited for a fairy princess. Your features are fine and delicate." George looked very closely at her face. "In fact, your eyes are a very interesting shade of gray."

"Interesting?" Harriet laughed. "Gray is the color of complete boredom."

"There is nothing boring about your eyes, Harriet." George looked completely serious. "I believe they are one of your finest features."

"Truly?" Harriet suddenly felt giddy as she stared back into George's eyes. "Yours are quite nice too."

"An odd color, do you not think?"

"But that is what makes them so grand. Original, I would say, completely original," Harriet said, still staring.

George coughed and looked away. "Thank you. Now returning to your choice of costume,"— George picked up his book—"why not dress as a character from one of your beloved Scott's books."

"That is a famous idea," Harriet said.

"I look forward to your choice."

"But what of your costume? What shall you wear?"

"I honestly have not given it much thought. Perhaps I should take my own advice and dress as a male character from Scott's book."

"You could be a knight," Harriet said quickly. "In fact, what say you if we both dressed as a character from *Ivanhoe*?"

"I say it is a splendid idea," George said.

"There are the Knights Templars and, of course, Ivanhoe masqueraded as the disinherited knight and wore black armor." Excited at the prospect of becoming characters from her favorite novel, Harriet forgot her insecurities and blurted, "How wonderful you would look as a knight."

"That settles it," George said. "For you, dear lady." He took her hand and brought it to his lips for a solemn kiss. It was made completely in jest, but even so, the thrill of his mouth upon her flesh nearly made her swoon.

She giggled nervously, but when he glanced up at her with his eyes resembling molten copper, her laughter quieted.

"Whose favor did Ivanhoe fight for?" George asked softly.

"The Lady Rowena's." Harriet dared not breathe.

"Was she as beautiful as you?"

Harriet's heart skipped a beat at hearing those words. In fact, George looked surprised for having said them. "Surely you jest, sirrah."

"Actually, I am completely in earnest. Harriet, tell me why I have taken so long to notice how lovely you are?"

Harriet panicked. George Clasby was paying her a compliment of the likes that she had only dreamed of hearing. She did not know what to do.

Yesterday they had said barely a few words and

today, George had become an expert at flattery. But of course he was well versed in compliments, she thought quickly. He had to be in order to earn his reputation with the ladies. But this was the first time he had ever graced her ears with such verbal flowers, and she reeled.

And then she cleared her throat.

"Harriet, I beg your pardon." He was quick with an apology. "I did not mean to make you feel uncomfortable."

"'Tis simply that I was gathering my thoughts in order to answer your question."

"I never should have posed it."

But she knew the answer. George had never noticed her before because he had always been too busy with his latest paramour. The latest *on-dit* was that George Clasby had indeed changed his ways. He was completely free from any entanglements with married women of society. Had she not heard from Artemis just this morning that he had rejected the attentions of Lady Ellerton?

Harriet swallowed hard. "Thank you, Mr. Clasby, for your kind compliment."

"Please," he said softly. "You must call me George. And Harriet, I am afraid your ice has melted," George pointed out.

"Indeed it has," Harriet said. She wiped her fingertips on a napkin. "I see Sally has returned. Our hour has passed."

"We did not read our first chapter."

"Perhaps when next you call, we can read *Ivanhoe* together. That way you will know exactly which character you will wish to be."

"Very well. I shall come by later this afternoon, if that is convenient."

"Indeed it is, Mr. Clasby—I mean, George."

George bought Sally an ice and left Gunter's to see the two ladies into their carriage. He did not quite understand what had come over him to pay such homage to Harriet's beauty. But he was glad that he had. Harriet positively glowed. Lud! The day before her father had accused him of improper advances!

Was it the fact that her father wanted him to drop dead that he felt compelled to woo Harriet? For that was exactly what he was doing, and if he did not tread carefully, he was bound to find himself in a heap of trouble.

He recalled the soft blushes on Harriet's cheeks when he looked at her. She was lovely, and in a way, George felt like a knight of old, unworthy to carry her favors without slaying a dragon somewhere. Was the dragon her father? He didn't think so; Harriet doted on her parents and they her.

He walked away from the confectioner's shop with his hands in his pockets. It was a long walk back to his town house, but he did not mind.

"Clasby," a man drawled with insolent pride.

George turned around. Lord Grafton was about to enter Gunter's. "Grafton, what an unpleasant surprise," he said cheerfully.

Grafton looked puzzled, as if he did not quite catch the jab. "I hear that you are on the Marriage Mart. Is that true?"

"Perhaps."

"Whitlow will never accept you. His blessings have already been given."

"So I understand."

"Just so you do," Grafton said with meaning. "Miss Whitlow is already spoken for."

It was then that George realized he had found his dragon. But he had to slay this one with utmost care.

Chapter Eight

*H*arriet checked her appearance in the glass before she left her bedchamber. She wore one of her newly altered gowns in hopes of impressing George. The soft blue muslin of her afternoon dress gave her eyes an even deeper gray shine. George had complimented her on her eyes and she intended to do what she could to keep him looking into them.

Her brown hair, wispy as always, would not stay tight in the upsweep of ringlets Sally had arranged just an hour before, but there was nothing to be done. She allowed the flyaway tendrils escaping the pins to have their way. With one last pinch to her cheeks to bring out color, she bent down to retrieve her beloved copy of *Ivanhoe* from her nightstand. This book would have entirely new meaning to her now that she shared the story with George.

Harriet skipped out of her bedchamber and quickly descended the main stairs only to feel her heart drop to her feet with disappointment. Lord

Grafton entered the foyer and handed his gloves and hat to the butler. She was sorely tempted to quietly turn and run back to her room, but Lord Grafton looked up and saw her.

"Miss Whitlow," he said.

"Lord Grafton." Harriet took the remaining steps slowly, dreading each one. She expected George at any moment. Her nerves tightened. She was in no mood for the two men to square off like a couple of roosters. "What a surprise."

"I hoped to speak with you privately," he said when she reached the bottom of the stairs.

Harriet swallowed hard and placed her hand upon Lord Grafton's offered arm. *Oh dear*, she lamented silently. "Shall we go into the drawing room?"

"And what have we here," Lord Grafton said in a tone that was patronizing and completely irritating. "Another book? Did you know that you will ruin your eyesight if you read too much?"

Harriet was quite certain that Lord Grafton believed only females could read too much. "I had never heard that, my lord."

"Just the same, perhaps you should heed my words. I hear you read quite a bit."

"How can one possibly read too much?" Harriet asked.

Lord Grafton was taken aback by her remark, but he ignored it completely and gestured for her to enter the room first.

Once seated, with Sally stationed in the far corner to play chaperone, Harriet asked, "Shall I ring for tea?"

"I cannot stay long."

Harriet held in the sigh of relief that threatened to escape. She sat down and waited quietly for Lord Grafton to share his news of importance. The longer it took for him to speak, the more dread she felt. She knew what he was about.

"Miss Whitlow," he began. "You must realize that I hold you in high regard." He stopped.

"Thank you, my lord," Harriet said quickly.

"I believe that our situations in life are quite of a similarity." He stopped for a deep breath as he bent down on one knee.

"Oh dear," Harriet whispered. She had to think of something, and fast.

"I have already received your father's blessing," he started.

Of course her father had given his blessing. Lord Grafton had been handpicked by her persnickety sire! Harriet rallied nearly twenty years of instruction on how to behave as a woman born to nobility. She gathered strength from that vast well of knowledge in order to remain calm. She had received proposals before, but never had a man captivated her father as much as Lord Grafton. She did what any proper miss would do in an awkward situation and screamed at the top of her lungs.

Lord Grafton was on his feet in a trice. "Miss Harriet, what is it?"

She pointed in the far corner. "A mouse! I am certain that I saw a mouse." This announcement caused Sally considerable distress and she also screamed and jumped up onto her chair.

Lord Grafton looked toward the ceiling and clenched his fists by his sides. He searched the area thoroughly to finally declare that he could find no such creature.

"I saw a small ball of gray whisk across the floor," Harriet said with a small measure of guilt in deceiving him. She told the truth, only it was no mouse, it was one of Sally's balls of yarn that rolled beneath the settee.

"Perhaps it was dust," Lord Grafton drawled.

"If it was, my mother will be after the servants." Harriet looked at Sally, who still stood on her chair.

"You may get down, Sally. Lord Grafton assures us there is no mouse."

Just then the Whitlow butler announced the arrival of George Clasby.

Oh no, Harriet thought. Lord Grafton had been put into a foul mood because of his interrupted proposal. The expression he wore when he saw Mr. Clasby was close to restrained fury. He even cast her a harsh glance. But it was worth it. Lord Grafton's proposal had been prevented. Harriet smiled. "Mr. Clasby, do come in and make yourself comfortable."

The two men eyed one another.

Fearing they might break into an exchange of heated words, Harriet nervously pulled the bell rope. "Would either of you care for tea?"

Lord Grafton cleared his throat. "Like I said before, I cannot stay. I shall see myself out."

"Very well," Harriet said with real relief. "Good day, my lord."

Lord Grafton did not appear to hear her. He stalked out without another word.

Harriet felt ashamed at her charade but very glad that he was gone. She had bought herself time, but not much. He would no doubt try again. She let out a weary sigh.

"Harriet," George whispered. "What is the matter?"

"Matter? Why nothing at all, whatever gives you the idea that anything is amiss?" Harriet slumped back into the high backed chair she had just vacated.

"You are agitated. Has Grafton insulted you or acted too warm?"

Harriet glanced at Sally, now settled back into her chair. She smiled over her needlework at Harriet. "Heavens no. He is simply a gentleman whose company I find tiresome."

"Indeed." George still looked concerned, but he sat down.

"Not to worry," Harriet said with a wave of her hand in dismissal. She pushed Lord Grafton out of her thoughts and turned to George. "Now have you given your costume any further consideration?"

"I have."

Harriet clapped her hands in excitement. "Then tell me, what will you wear?"

"That, my dear, is a surprise," George said. "First, I must find out if my tailor is able to accommodate my choice. And what of you? What costume will you choose?"

"*Tsk, tsk.*" Harriet grinned. "If you will not tell, then neither shall I."

"Playing hard to get?"

"I take my lead from you."

"Then I must use great care in how I influence you in future."

"Indeed." Harriet said with a giggle. "But are you trying to influence me for good or for evil?"

"I do not believe in evil, Miss Whitlow," George said with a lofty air of arrogance matching Lord Grafton's usual tone.

Harriet laughed, thinking he was joking. "Surely you jest."

"Actually I do not," George said with a shrug of his shoulders. "I do not hold with the belief of an evil force fighting against a good one. I think people are generally good at heart. They merely make poor choices."

Harriet felt her eyebrows rise in shock. "But George, do you not attend church services? The scriptures are quite clear that evil *does* exist."

George looked away. "I am not a religious man."

Harriet did not respond because the tea cart arrived. She expertly poured for them both and offered a dish to her maid, her mind working furiously for the proper words. Stirring sugar and milk into her tea, she asked, "But what of all the terrible things people do to one another? How do explain those?"

"People choose to do what they do," George said with a shrug. He sipped his tea.

"But *why* do they do what they do? Why would a person choose to do wrong instead of right?"

George considered the question carefully. "I believe it is because there is something to lose or gain."

"So you believe people are motivated by purely materialistic desires?"

"Perhaps. Actually, I have never truly considered the depth of such a question before. I am not one to dwell on the miseries of life and their causes. I prefer to surround myself with pleasantries. It appears you have given such matters much thought and I commend you for it."

George's compliment sounded too much like the desire to end the conversation. But Harriet did not wish to stop.

He did not appear offended by her remarks and she was grateful for that. He gave her a smile, but in his eyes she read something close to admiration, and that gave her courage. "If I may ask you to consider this one question, I shall let the topic drop," she started. "If there is no good versus evil, if you will, no need to give over our sinful natures to God, then what is the point of trying to better oneself?"

"Hmmm," George rubbed his chin. "Well, for one, I do believe society shapes us. For instance, the *ton* demonstrates its power over behavior by the threat of ostracism from the very society men and women of means seek approval."

"Ah, but that does not explain a person's kindness merely for the sake of giving or being kind with no hope of repayment. Nor does it give any motive for those who continually do wrong. For all the rules society portrays, many of them are overlooked if the perpetrators are not found out."

"Ah yes, discretion being the most important virtue to the haute monde." George looked as if he knew all too well the results of indiscretion. "Even so, many have done wrong hidden behind the purpose of good, behind the mask of religion even."

"Indeed," Harriet said. "An even more difficult motivation to understand."

"Exactly so," George agreed.

"But a perfect preface to our story. *Ivanhoe* deals with some of these very same issues." She held up the leather-bound book.

"Then delay no longer," George said. "Let us delve into your book and debate the mysteries of human nature later."

Harriet smiled sweetly at him. "I completely agree."

George leaned his head against the high backed chair. He closed his eyes and listened to her deep soft voice reading the words of her beloved Sir Walter Scott. She had impressed him with her sharp intellect. He had no idea such interesting thoughts danced inside her pretty head. No wonder she was respected. She lived what she believed with true conviction.

Unlike him. . . .

He had used women and allowed them to use him. For what gain, he wondered? He had not lined his pockets with anything more than a few trinkets, and yet he had returned to his folly time and again, knowing full well that it would eventually spell his doom. Why had he gone to such lengths when what he truly desired was to be loved and cherished for always?

Was there such a thing as an evil nature that had spurred him on into folly? He did not like to think so, but then why had each encounter with a woman left him feeling emptier than before?

When his parents had died, his elder brother by nearly fourteen years had in effect raised him. His brother was strict, pious even, but he offered no answers to the questions posed by an eleven-year-old boy. Soon, George had refused to acknowledge a God who would abandon him in such a manner.

But George knew he wanted what others had—what Ashbourne had with his lady-wife and even what Artemis and her Lord Cherrington possessed. Could he find what he had been looking for all this time from the respectable slip of a girl who read to him? She was above his touch in so many ways. She was near perfection and displayed such sweet innocence that he felt like a filthy rag in her presence.

Harriet read until she feared George had fallen asleep. When she gently closed the book, his eyes snapped open instantly.

"Why have you stopped?" he asked.

"It grows late," Harriet said. "My parents should be home soon and we are expected at the Collingtons' for supper."

"I should be on my way, then." He stood but appeared hesitant to leave.

Harriet felt a shiver pass down her spine as she looked into his coppery eyes. She wanted so much to share how full her heart was at the moment, but she could do nothing. Her lips refused to form the words. Instead, she sputtered. "Shall we meet again tomorrow? We can read." She lifted *Ivanhoe*.

"Very well, I shall call the same time tomorrow." George still did not leave. "Tomorrow night there is a ball held by the Duke and Duchess of Tyre—"

"Will you be there?" Harriet asked quickly.

"I will, in fact, by a rather late invitation." George kicked at the corner of the carpet. "Thank you for, uh, reading to me."

"It has been my pleasure. Now you understand the draw of Scott."

"Indeed, I do. And I must beg your forgiveness if I offended you when we spoke earlier."

Harriet cocked her head to the side. "You have not offended me in the least. And do not worry. Regardless of what you believe, I pray for your soul," Harriet said lightly, almost in jest, but the truth of the matter was that she had been doing just that for ages.

George looked startled by her admission but not displeased. "Then perhaps there is hope for me," he said with a smile. "Until tomorrow then."

"Until then." Harriet walked him to the door just as her parents arrived. They exchanged pleasantries before George left but her father wore a deep frown.

"Mr. Clasby came to tea, Father. And do not worry. Sally was with us." She kissed his cheek.

"Did Lord Grafton drop by?" her father asked.

"Indeed he did." Harriet grew wary. What if her father asked about Lord Grafton's proposal?

"He has asked permission to collect you for the ball at the Tyres'. I have agreed."

Harriet high spirits sank. "You are not going?" She looked at both her parents.

"Not this time. But Grafton will accompany you."

Harriet stood speechless as her mother caressed her cheek before heading up the main staircase. Her father disappeared into his study. She took a step toward her father's study, but her courage faltered. What could she say? What if her father refused to accept her heart's choice? What then? Her father could very well forbid her from seeing George again, and then everything would have been for naught.

She had prevented Lord Grafton from proposing today, but if she accompanied him to a ball, he would surely try again. If she said no, would it carry any weight with her parents? Her father believed Lord Grafton the perfect match, and he intensely disliked George.

George had just begun to show signs of real interest but she saw no hope of him winning over her father anytime soon. Or at least in time to change her father's mind about Lord Grafton.

She had to do something, anything, to keep Lord Grafton from uttering another proposal.

Chapter Nine

*H*arriet paced the floor of her bedchamber. She saw no feasible way out of going to the ball with Lord Grafton. Her parents had made other plans. If she wished to attend the Tyre ball held a mere two blocks away from the Whitlow town house, she must go accompanied by Lord Grafton in his open carriage for one and all to see.

Arriving alone on Lord Grafton's arm was as good as an announcement that his suit was blessed by her parents. To be so entrusted with their daughter for an evening out spoke volumes. But even worse was her fear that he might propose once again.

She racked her brain for ideas to keep him from doing so in order to avoid having to say no to him. It would be much easier to face her father if she could explain that a proposal had never truly been made. In fact it would be far better for all parties involved. She could hardly imagine that any man would take rejection lightly. She simply could not allow Lord Grafton to ask for her hand.

She continued to pace. She would do Lord Grafton a good service if she kept him from uttering those terrible words that would no doubt seal her fate.

She stopped pacing and looked at her reflection in the mirror. She would not marry him. She would simply refuse. Surely her father would not drag her to the altar, would he? Her father was a stubborn man, she knew, especially when he firmly believed he was in the right. But Harriet also knew that she could never marry Lord Grafton. Not when she loved George Clasby. And she loved him, deeply and irrevocably.

The previous two Seasons, her father had protected her from having to refuse a gentleman's offer directly to his face. Instead, she had given her polite answer of needing to discuss the matter with her father. Her father had delivered her rejection to the gentlemen over friendly glasses of port. But she did not think her father would allow her to turn Lord Grafton away so easily.

Sally peeked her head into the room. "Miss Harriet, Lord Grafton is here."

Harriet chewed her bottom lip. "Very well. I might as well get this over with," she muttered.

"Don't worry, Miss Harriet. It'll all work out right in the end, you'll see," her maid encouraged her. "Your papa will come around in time."

"Do you truly think so?" Harriet wanted to believe that, but what if he did not? What if her father forbade her to marry George? She shook her head. First things first. She had to keep Lord Grafton from proposing. Finding a way to make

George propose, much less convince her father to allow it, must be dealt with later.

"Of course I do," Sally said with a wink. She knew which man Harriet favored.

"I do hope you have the right of it," Harriet whispered as she exited her room.

Harriet walked slowly down the hall, dragging each step, wishing she did not have to face this. At the stairs, she spotted Lord Grafton standing in the foyer talking to her father. The two looked amused, and for a fleeting moment, Harriet wished that she had never met George Clasby. How easy it would be if she cared for Lord Grafton instead. And how proud she would make her father. Instead, she was bound to disappoint him.

"Ah, Harriet, there you are." Her father smiled up at her.

"Here I am," she muttered. She descended the stairs until she stood before them. "Good evening, Lord Grafton."

"Miss Whitlow." He bowed and offered her his arm, and in no time they were climbing into his shiny new curricle with the Grafton crest on the side.

The night air was mild and Lord Grafton was careful to drive slowly as they rounded the corner onto Park Lane.

"Lord Grafton," Harriet started what she planned to be a barrage of chatter that would last until they arrived at the ball. "I have looked in several medical journals that were my brother's—he studied medicine for a time, and I could find no references to poor eyesight as a result of extensive reading."

" 'Tis a turn of phrase, Miss Whitlow."

"Indeed, but I feel compelled to assure you that my eyesight is in no danger."

"Miss Whitlow, I wonder if—"

"Oh," Harriet quickly interrupted. "I must beg your pardon for yesterday's mouse. You were correct. There was no mouse at all. I mistook an oddly shaped ball of gray yarn that Sally had dropped for a furry creature as it rolled beneath her chair."

"No apologies needed, Miss Whitlow."

Harriet stared into the streets illuminated by the glow of gaslights. She had to keep talking. "Are you enjoying the Season, my lord?"

"Yes," Lord Grafton answered. "The reason I have come to London is to find—"

"Oh!" Harriet pointed. "Do look. There is Lord and Lady Cherrington!" Harriet waved furiously. "Did you know that Lord Cherrington is an expert swordsman?"

"Uh, no," Lord Grafton stuttered.

Harriet noticed that the knuckles of his hands had turned white as he gripped the reins. Even so, she kept up a constant stream of one-sided conversation until finally they pulled into the Tyre drive, which was miraculously empty save one carriage ahead of them. They would not have a long wait, which meant she was in the clear. Lord Grafton would hardly propose in the driveway. She was indeed safe.

When they entered the main hall to give their

outer garments to the Tyre butler, Harriet said nothing and neither did Lord Grafton. He looked unsettled, as if he had just been through a storm. Harriet smiled. Her plan had worked, for now. She wished he would realize that they had nothing in common. Lord Grafton needed to search out a bride elsewhere to bear his heirs.

Harriet did not mistake the raised brows of the duke and duchess as they reached out their hands in welcome. Harriet's arrival without her parents was duly noted and would no doubt be the subject of gossip on the morrow.

Lord Grafton's purpose in escorting her was clear but Harriet was prepared. She was not about to risk dancing a waltz with Lord Grafton during which they would have a chance to talk privately. She would concede only to fast dances that kept partners separated and switching places often.

They entered the ballroom and Harriet's hand rested lightly upon Lord Grafton's arm. She could not bolt just yet. They both nodded to several acquaintances, stopping to chat for a few moments at a time, until finally Harriet felt she could excuse herself.

"Lord Grafton," Harriet said softly. "I must beg your leave to find the room set aside for the ladies."

A slight flush to his cheek made it clear that he understood where she was headed. "Of course."

Harriet made her escape. She glanced around until she saw her friends. She made her way quickly through the crowded ballroom. "Artemis," she breathed.

"Harriet," Artemis said. "This is turning into a sad crush. I doubt we shall stay long." Her arm was lovingly linked with her tall husband's.

"There will be no room to dance," Lord Cherrington said with a frown.

"They have not yet opened the other doors." Harriet pointed to two sets of doors that kept the other half of the ballroom closed off.

Artemis leaned close. "I noticed that you arrived with Lord Grafton."

Harriet rolled her eyes. "My father arranged it, I am afraid. I found out at the last moment. Needless to say, the trip here was terribly uncomfortable."

"How so?" Artemis asked. Her eyes opened wide. "Do not say that Lord Grafton proposed!"

"He is looking for the opportunity but I have done my best to prevent the question from coming up in the conversation," Harriet said.

Lord Cherrington chuckled. "Perhaps you should be more bold. Lord Grafton strikes me as a man who misses subtlety."

"What do you mean?"

"Most men know when their attentions are unwanted. He seems quite determined to have you regardless of your wishes. Perhaps you need to take a more forthright approach."

"You see, I cannot refuse him outright as it may not carry any weight with my father. I must prevent him from proposing," Harriet said.

He shrugged his shoulders. " 'Tis merely a thought."

"A good one," Artemis said with an encouraging pat on her husband's hand.

Harriet saw Lord Grafton making his way toward them. She had not even made it to the necessary. She bade her friends good evening and ducked behind them, trying to stay out of Lord Grafton's view. Perhaps Cherry had the right of it. Lord Grafton did not seem to understand that she did not welcome his courtship. She needed to do something bold.

The Lord helps those who help themselves. The curate's voice once again sifted through her thoughts.

Harriet scanned the room until her gaze stopped on a dark red head bowing over a classic featured blonde who made her come-out this Season. Harriet could not remember the girl's name but something inside her splintered as she watched George Clasby bow and scrape over that feminine hand. The blonde gazed adoringly up at George while her mama looked on, completely unconcerned.

George had made definite improvement to his reputation while calling on her. She stood there, watching George with the attractive blonde, and it bothered her very much that the wonderful times spent in George's company enabled him to woo others on the Marriage Mart.

A rare streak of jealousy seared her insides. She was more than frustrated. She had been trying to prevent the man she did not want from proposing while the man she did want fawned over another.

Again, Harriet wished that she did not have a sterling reputation. It was, after all, her much sought after respectability that had landed her in this coil!

George looked up then and caught her glare. She did not bother to look away. He bowed quickly over the blonde's hand and whispered something that brought a smile to the girl's lips. But Harriet felt some relief when George walked away from her.

He then made his way through the crowded ballroom until he stood before her. "Good evening, Miss Whitlow," he said. "Is anything amiss?"

"Actually." She bit her lower lip. "Yes, yes there is something amiss indeed." An idea dawned on her that might solve the problem of Lord Grafton. It was definitely bold and she hoped she had the nerve for it.

The Lord helps those who help themselves.

"Then might I be of assistance?" He tipped his head.

She leaned close and whispered near his ear, "I fear I must impose on our friendship and ask if you would be so kind as to help me find the room reserved for convenience?"

He laughed softly as if she were joking. "Have you not been here before?"

"I have, but I have forgotten. It is such a sad crush that I fear it will take much too long to make it to the room that is clear across the floor and near the main entrance. There must one on this side of the house, perhaps the first floor?"

"Of course." He offered his arm.

Harriet took it with relief. She need only be gone with George for an undetermined amount of time and surely it would be remarked upon. She looked at George next to her who appeared completely at ease. She could think of no other excuse to get him alone and away from the main room.

They need only be seen leaving the ballroom together then returning much later and her reputation would be marred just a little. Lord Grafton would hopefully be furious enough to give up on her completely. And if George suffered a slight setback to his own image reparations, then even better for her. She did not want a bevy of newly out innocents vying for his attention now that he was well on his way back to society's good graces.

They left through an opened door that led to a dimly lit hallway filled with portraits on the walls. "Which way do you think?" George asked. "It has been an age since I was here last."

"Perhaps at the end of this hall," Harriet said.

They checked two doors. One revealed a small study and the other, a room set aside for billiards. George's eyes widened with interest when he looked upon the gaming table.

"Care to play?" Harriet teased.

"I would love to, but we must find the water closet and return as quickly as possible before our absence is noticed."

"Yes, of course," Harriet said quickly. "Do you have a billiards room at your country house?"

"I do," George said. "It is a rather modest home really, but comfortable."

"And modern, I would wager."

He grinned. "I have upgraded where I could to the best of my ability. And you should never wager, my dear. Gambling leads to all sorts of evil vice," he teased with a wink.

"Of course not. A turn of phrase," Harriet said. "But if I were to hazard a guess, it would be that you have tinkered extensively, except perhaps for the heated water for your bath."

He laughed then said, "I will find a way yet, you shall see." They headed up the stairs to the first floor and checked another room that proved to be a vacant bedchamber. "You are correct, I have made changes to just about everything."

She hoped to see the changes he had made. "Are your lands extensive?" Harriet asked. She enjoyed hearing about his home and the genuine pleasure in his voice when he described it.

"Quite vast. I have tenant farmers who do wonders with both crops and livestock. It is a beautiful old heap, really. I think you would like it."

"It sounds divine," Harriet whispered.

"Ah, I think we might have found it," George said as he opened the door to a small room with a tiled floor.

Harriet stepped into the room quickly. "I shall only be a moment," she said before shutting the door.

George nodded. She noticed that his ears were slightly red at the tops and she knew she had embarrassed him by asking for his escort.

Harriet took her time. Fascinated by a pump on a stand with a long pipe running up toward the ceiling, she tested it. The duke and duchess had running water! Or rather, they had taken the very same principle of the water closet to draw fresh water into a bowl with a hole at the bottom and a rubber stopper.

She must tell George to have a look as soon as she was finished. She washed her hands in the basin and Lord Cherrington's advice suddenly came to mind. She had effectively taken a bold, even improper action, by asking George to escort her. Perhaps she needed to do something even more drastic to guarantee Lord Grafton's surrender and retreat.

As she dried her hands, she remembered Lord Grafton's reaction to Miss Bronwell's attempts to capture his interest and another idea dawned. Quickly, she lifted her filmy skirt, unfastened and wiggled out of her pantalettes. She then pulled up her chemise and tucked it underneath her corset as best she could so that the lace edge hit the tops of her thighs instead of her knees.

She twisted the pantalettes into a neat little ball and shoved the fabric into her pocket. She saw how her skirt bulged noticeably and realized she would have to find a place to hide them before they returned to the ballroom.

She had to hurry.

Miss Bronwell had not worn a shift when she fell into the Collingtons' pond last year and she had been forgiven. Surely Harriet Whitlow would be given the same grace if she dampened her gown just a little so that it clung to her bare legs.

Lord Grafton would surely kick up dust and

leave her alone for good. Her gown was made of fine muslin and would no doubt cling nicely. She moved quickly, the speed of her actions blocking out all doubt or second thoughts. She had to be bold. She had no choice!

George tapped his foot with impatience. Harriet was taking forever and he could do nothing but wait. Finally the door opened and a sheepish looking Harriet walked out.

"I beg your pardon for being so long. You must have a look in there," she said. "His Grace has a small pump installed for running water into a basin that has a drain. The water must come from a cistern hidden in the attics, much like the water closet itself."

George shook his head. "Another time perhaps. We must get back."

"I had to see how the pump worked. Perhaps you could install something similar at your Trent Hall."

George smiled. "Perhaps." He could easily imagine her testing the thing over and over. Regardless of his piqued interest in the Duke and Duchess of Tyre's plumbing, he had to get them both back to the ball before they were missed.

He offered her his arm and they descended the stairs. Once again in the hallway, she pulled away and entered the billiards room.

"Harriet," he said nervously from the doorway. If they were caught wandering about alone it would be a compromising situation to say the least. "I really think we should return to the ballroom."

"Not even one game?" she asked.

"Not one." George wondered what she was about. She knew better than to drag her feet. They darted back into the ballroom with no one the wiser, until George caught Jory DeVillars looking their way from nearby.

George nodded, but his heart sank when DeVillars smirked and quickly raised and lowered his eyebrows. George shook his head emphatically. How could he possibly explain to DeVillars that he was helping Harriet find the privy without bringing further ridicule down upon his ears?

"Are you spoken for the supper dance, Mr. Clasby?" Harriet asked.

He had purposefully saved it for her, but after seeing her arrive with Grafton, he wondered why she would ask. "I am not. Are you? You did come with Lord Grafton."

"My father's doing, not mine," she whispered.

He was kept from remarking upon the matter when the very object of their conversation appeared before them just as the other half of the ballroom was opened to the sounds of the orchestra playing a quadrille.

"Miss Whitlow, I should like the first dance." Grafton's lips formed a tight line. He did not look pleased in the least.

George did not like the man's tone, which was the bark of an order instead of a request. "Now see here, Grafton."

"I have been looking for Miss Whitlow for some time now. When I finally find her she is in your jaded company," he nearly growled. "Her father shall hear of this, I assure you."

Harriet stepped between them. "Lord Grafton," she said smoothly even though George read the nervousness in her eyes. "Come, I will dance with you."

George watched Grafton lead her onto the dance floor and they joined their set. He also noticed something about Harriet he had not noticed before.

"A bit transparent, ain't she?" DeVillars whispered in his ear. "Ah, but she has lovely limbs."

George stared transfixed at Harriet's gown, as it clung indecently to her legs. It was quite true; she had beautifully shaped legs, their outline clear as crystal when she turned just right and the light shown from behind her. Confound it! She was not wearing anything under her skirt!

George turned quickly to face DeVillars. "Do not say another word," he said fiercely.

DeVillars walked away with a knowing smile that George knew he would have to address later. He looked around to see if anyone else had noticed Harriet's indiscretion of fashion, but he could not tell. Surely she did not arrive this way, or perhaps she did but he had not noticed. He had been too busy making his rounds.

George did not wish to wait for the dance to end, but he could hardly interrupt them and bring unwanted attention toward Harriet. When Grafton finally escorted Harriet to the sidelines of the dance floor, George moved toward them.

"Stay right here," Grafton said gruffly. "I shall fetch our wraps."

George watched him walk away. "Harriet," he

whispered. "I must talk to you. Might we make our way toward the entrance hall?"

"Certainly." Her voice was dull, her eyes nearly sullen.

"Are you all right?" he asked gently.

"I think I may have made a grave error."

George breathed easier. Thank goodness she realized she was missing her undergarments. "Did you forget something when you dressed this evening?"

She looked confused.

He pointedly looked down at her skirt and noticed it looked a little damp. Is that what had taken her so long? She had been dampening her skirts?

Harriet blushed a thousand shades of red. "Yes, that must be it. I must have forgotten," she stuttered.

He could not find it in his heart to question her further, nor did he have the time. Grafton came toward her with her pelisse, and quickly wrapped it around her shoulders. Grafton, too, had noticed, and he looked angry as a thundercloud.

"I can take her home," George said when they reached the entry. He did not care for the grave frown on Grafton's face, nor the sweeping look of accusation, as if Harriet's appearance was somehow his fault.

"That will not be necessary." Grafton's tone was at the height of arrogance. "Lord Whitlow entrusted his daughter to my care alone this evening. I will see her home."

George had to agree that it would look dashed

awkward if she arrived with Grafton and left with him. But he did not care for Grafton's mood one bit. He glanced at Harriet.

"I do have the headache and 'tis dreadful," she said. "Thank you for your kind offer, Mr. Clasby. I shall be just fine. Do not worry."

"Indeed," George said, but he could not help but worry for her. "Have a care," he warned. He looked straight at Grafton, who merely nodded before escorting a miserable-looking Harriet out of the door.

Harriet sat in silence next to a furious Lord Grafton. She needn't worry about him proposing. She had done exactly what she sought out to do, but she had not expected to feel this terribly for having accomplished her goal. To make matters even worse, she had lied to George.

She sank farther into the seat, remembering the shock that registered in Lord Grafton's eyes when he noticed that her skirt had clung to her legs. Her moment of victory was dashed to defeat when she saw just how transparent the muslin had become in the bright lights of the ballroom. She revealed far more than she had intended. She looked positively indecent.

Her head ached and pounded in earnest as she sat next to a coldly silent Lord Grafton. She had made a complete fool of herself and no doubt the pompous Lord Grafton would take pleasure in telling her father exactly what he thought of her. And then she would be in deep suds. Her father would not be fooled for an instant and she would surely be punished, perhaps even sent home before the Season was over.

She chanced a glance at Lord Grafton. His mouth had thinned into a hard line. "Lord Grafton," she squeaked. What could she possibly say?

"Do not attempt to explain your behavior this evening, Miss Whitlow. It was beyond the pale and beneath a woman of your character."

"But—"

"Let us never again speak of it." He pulled in front of the Whitlow town house. Silently he offered her his hand to assist her in getting out of the carriage. As soon as her feet hit the pavement, he released her hand as if he feared he might catch some terrible disease from her.

Still, he walked her to the front door, stiff disapproval reeking from him. "Good evening, Miss Whitlow," he finally said with a disgusted curl of his lip when he spoke her name.

"Thank you, Lord Grafton." He turned to leave and Harriet quickly added, "I beg your pardon, but I do hope you understand. I mean, you need not tell my father."

"That is something I must think on." He climbed back into his curricle and left.

Harriet stepped into the quiet and empty hall with an invisible stone of regret hanging about her neck. Whatever did she think would happen when she decided to take off her cursed pantalettes? That was the problem. She had not taken the time to think the matter through. Instead she boldly charged ahead without a thought to the consequences that might lie ahead.

The butler spied her just as she walked into the hall. He raised his eyebrow, surprised to see her home so soon.

"The headache," she quickly explained. She wrapped her pelisse around her and ran up the stairs to her room.

Once inside her bedchamber, she threw off her covering and lit every lamp in her room. She fervently hoped that it was not nearly as bad as she thought. Holding her breath, she looked into the mirror and shuddered. It was far worse. The outline of her legs was indeed clear—far too clear for decency's sake.

And then she remembered that she had stuffed her pantalettes behind the pillows in the billiard room. She forgot to retrieve them before she left.

"Oh no!" She fell onto her bed with an anguished cry. She was ruined!

Chapter Ten

*H*arriet rang for her maid and waited. How could she have been so stupid as to leave her undergarments at the ball! She heard the light scratch on the door before it opened.

"Sally," Harriet said. "I need you to do me a great favor of service."

Sally's eyes widened. "Certainly, Miss Harriet. What is it?"

"You have a friendly acquaintance with the Duchess of Tyre's personal maid do you not?"

"That I do. She's my cousin."

"If I were to send you to her on an errand, will you promise to be discreet and never ever tell a soul?"

Sally's eyes grew wide. "A mystery."

"Can you keep a secret?" Harriet asked.

" 'Course. You can trust me, Miss Harriet."

Harriet nodded. Sally had been in her father's household a very long time and Harriet did indeed trust her. She had been her lady's maid since she left the schoolroom. "I left my pantalettes in the billiards room behind the pillows on the sofa at tonight's ball," she said quickly.

Sally's eyes opened even wider.

"Please do not look so shocked," Harriet whispered. "I simply forgot to retrieve them."

"Beggin' your pardon Miss Harriet, but surely you did not lose them because . . ." Sally's cheeks were aflame in embarrassment.

"Heavens no!" Harriet's hand flew to her neck, horrified that her maid would think such a thing of her. "Certainly not. Oh Sally, I did something terrible though. I purposely took off my pantalettes knowing my gown would cling to my legs and that would chase Lord Grafton away once and for all."

Sally looked a little confused. "Seeing as how you took them off for him, I don't understand why he'd take offense."

Harriet smiled. It sounded ridiculous no matter how she explained it. "But he did take dreadful offense and well, it is a rather long story. If those pantalettes are found, I fear what might happen. Could you try to slip into the room unnoticed and bring them back?"

"Tonight?"

"It is very important. See if your cousin will give you a tour of the first floor or better yet, tell her I lost something in the billiards room, tell her whatever you think you must, only do not tell her exactly what I left behind. Promise you will slip in and out as quickly as possible."

Sally hesitated.

"I shall send a footman with you and something

for Her Grace from my mother who could not attend the ball. Please, please say you will do it," Harriet fairly begged. "I am desperately in need of your assistance."

"I will do it." Sally smiled.

Harriet sat wrapped in a blanket in her chair before a dying fire with a cup of warmed milk, but nothing helped the gnawing worry that she was indeed ruined. Sally returned, after what seemed like ages, to regrettably announce that her undergarments were not behind the pillow, not under the couch, nor anywhere in the billiards room. They were gone.

She did not know what to do. Her parents had arrived home and turned in early, thank goodness. She had told her mother that she had a dreadful headache and that accounted for why Lord Grafton brought her home early. Her mother had ordered the warmed milk and kissed her forehead, leaving Harriet to worry the night away.

The next morning dawned gray and dreary. Rain was pelting the windows when George finally woke and he rolled over with a groan. After Harriet had left, he had stayed at the Tyre ball to dance with several ladies into the wee hours. No matter how hard he tried to appreciate each woman's charms, they did not compare favorably when measured against Harriet's. It was simply no use. There could be no one but Harriet for him.

He had several errands to complete his costume

for tomorrow's masquerade. Hearing the patter of rain, he did not look forward to traveling about town in such a downpour.

He wondered what Harriet's costume would be. Would she choose the regal Rowena, whose father did not approve of her true love, or the noble Rebecca, who demonstrated honor in the face of prejudice?

He smiled when he thought of how pretty she would look as either character. The image of her shapely legs seen through her skirt the previous evening assaulted his thoughts with almost uncomfortable clarity. He had to admit he had enjoyed the view, but he hoped she did not suffer any ill remarks from her displayed limbs.

He hoped that he and Grafton had gotten her out of the ballroom before anyone had noticed. Anyone besides Jory DeVillars! George knew he would need to deal with that rakehell today to put a cork in the gentleman's big mouth.

He chuckled low as he thought of Harriet's reaction. She had forgotten to don her undergarments. What on earth could have been weighing so heavily upon her mind that caused her to overlook such a thing? He would no doubt find out this afternoon when he called upon her.

By the time George finished his toilette and left his town house, it was nearly noon. The rain had settled into a cold drizzle that shrouded the city in misty gloom. His first stop would be to his tailor and then perhaps the theatrical district. He could not simply wear a tunic and consider it good enough to be a Knight Templar. The theater would no doubt have something for him to wear. His black knee breeches would have to do for his leggings, but he must find something to pass as mail.

After shopping for an hour or two, George stopped at Boodle's for a spot of food and drink before making his rounds of calls upon the ladies he had danced with at the Tyre Ball. He had always saved Harriet for last. He managed to stay longer, especially now that they read *Ivanhoe* together. It was definitely something he looked forward to.

He took a seat at his favorite table and ordered a slab of roasted beef. In no time, several gentlemen had gathered round and as usual, the chatter led to gossip.

"I hear Lucinda Bronwell may have finally made a good match," one of the men started. "An old gent, but one with very deep pockets."

"You don't say," George said.

"She is a jewel that one, but cold. Her eyes shine hard as sapphires if you look into them. And a grand schemer, if you ask me. She would marry the devil himself if he paid high enough for her. She might as well have held an auction."

"She's a poor girl, Freddie," George said, thinking how Harriet would have responded. "With several younger siblings to think of."

"Aye, but she's as good as sold her dignity," Freddie said with a huff.

"Speaking of dignity." Jory DeVillars joined the table. "How goes your journey toward respectability, Clasby?"

"Quite well," George answered. "In fact, I believe I like living my life with nothing to feel guilty over come the next morning."

"Surprised us all, you have," Freddie said.

"You have called on many a young lady," one of the men pointed out. "My sister says Lydia Lawler has quite set her heart on you," he continued.

"Oh, but Clasby is after a much bigger fish in our London pond of love," Jory DeVillars purred. "One with quite a lovely tail, I might add." He winked at George.

"Careful, Jory," George warned. He felt his hackles rising. He knew he'd have to deal with DeVillars' insolence after his insinuations last night, but he had planned to speak to the man privately. George did not understand Jory's insidious need to irritate him in front of everyone.

"Well, spill it man," a gentleman cried. "Who is the lady?"

"Why our own Miss Harriet Whitlow," DeVillars supplied.

"Miss Whitlow?" a couple men said together in surprise.

"Has her father given his approval?" Freddie asked.

"My situation with Miss Whitlow is my own concern, gentlemen." George took a sip of his ale. "It is not to be spoken of in front of all of you." George pierced DeVillars with a look of warning to keep quiet.

"Of course it is and you know it. We always

talk about the ladies. But I thought she was as good as promised to Grafton," Freddie said.

"She was," DeVillars said with a grin. "But Clasby here is the fellow with whom she chose to roam the halls of Tyre House last night."

"DeVillars, I'll have you stop right there unless you'd like me to box your attic." The tops of George's ears were on fire but it was no good. Once that tidbit of juicy news was let out, the men couldn't hold back.

"By Jove, you don't say!" Freddie grinned.

"You were alone with Miss Whitlow? Give it up, man, what happened?" another cried.

George took a cheroot and lit the end from the candle on his table. Taking a deep puff, he ignored the question. One more lewd insinuation by De-Villars and he'd stamp the burning end out on the man's face.

"Very touchy," DeVillars teased. "You are indeed in a foul mood, Clasby." DeVillars leaned toward the other men seated around the table. "I do believe the infamous George Clasby has finally fallen to the charms of an innocent. But then perhaps she is not quite so innocent now."

That ended it! George was up and out of his chair so fast that he knocked it over to crash upon the floor. He flicked aside his cheroot unconcerned and it fell to the floor still lit.

"How dare you?" George grabbed hold of De-Villars' cravat and shirtfront. He fairly lifted the lighter man off the ground as he forced him up against the opposite wall. "Badger me all you want but kindly leave Miss Whitlow's good name alone."

"You've muddied it and you know it," De-Villars hissed.

George reared back and planted a solid square fist into the man's nose and then all hell broke loose. The rest of the men, staring in surprised shock, got up from the table to break up the fight that threatened to become an all-out rough and tumble. Freddie held George back and when he did, DeVillars leveled a facer that caught George on the cheek.

"Let go of me," George howled.

"You'll get us all thrown out of here if you do not stop this nonsense at once. The two of you are beginning to draw a crowd," Freddie hissed in George's ear.

George put up his hands in surrender until Freddie let go. George adjusted his own disheveled cravat, all the while glaring at DeVillars.

Freddie and the other gentlemen chased their audience away and reassured the manager that no harm had been done.

"You have some explaining to do, Jory." George righted his overturned chair.

"Nay, I think it is you who must explain. Explain this." DeVillars pulled out and unfolded a pair of white linen pantalettes embroidered along the hem and adorned with lace.

"What the devil are those?" George asked.

"Don't pretend you do not recognize them. They came from the Tyre house, the billiards room to be exact. I found them last night after you and Miss Whitlow took your stroll."

"Come on now, Jory, that is not in the least bit amusing," Freddie said.

"Of course not and I do not jest. We, as gentlemen, should not allow Clasby to get away with this. Dallying with married ladies is one thing, but harassing an innocent is completely unacceptable."

"They could be anyone's," one man said.

"Proves nothing," another added.

"Ah, but George knows, don't you? Miss Whitlow arrived quite respectable, but after she left the ballroom with you, she returned sans a vital undergarment." He shook the lace-edged pantalettes. "Which made her dress positively transparent when she danced."

For a moment George was struck speechless. He remembered clearly how Harriet had looked while she danced. But she said she had forgotten her undergarment.

"Notice the initials sewn so delicately. H. W." DeVillars paused for effect then went on. "I found them in the billiards room, behind a pillow on the couch. Could that have been the location of your deflowering?"

Seeing red, George lunged back at DeVillars and the two fell to the floor. "Blast your eyes, I did not touch her!" They rolled and wrestled but George managed to pummel him once or twice before the men pulled him off DeVillars.

Breathing heavily, George said, "Name your seconds, DeVillars!"

DeVillars stood, brushed off his coat, and tucked the delicate undergarment back into his inside pocket.

"Name them," George said again.

"Fighting for her honor?" DeVillars drawled.

"Her honor is completely safe and intact. She needs no defense, but you, sir, need to be taught a lesson in gentlemanly conduct that I will gladly administer. Meet me tomorrow morning at dawn on Primrose Hill! Freddie will act as one of my seconds; you can give the names to him."

"Now see here," Freddie started, "this has gone far enough."

"Not nearly," George said furiously. But inside his gut something disturbing twisted and turned. He kept revisiting the vision of Harriet darting quickly into the billiards room after they had found the water closet. "I bid you good day, gentlemen."

George stalked out into the cool wet air but his anger did not subside. Tomorrow morning he'd meet a man he had once called friend because of Harriet's undergarments. He felt no fear. He was not about to kill DeVillars, just disarm him. George was a much better shot, besides.

What bothered George more was that he had been lied to. Harriet had lied! She had not forgotten her undergarments; she had purposefully taken them off. But to what aim? He did not like to think Harriet capable of such ploys. He had had his fill with games of deception from the matrons of the haute monde pulling him in every manner of directions. He had been used to make

husbands jealous, he had been used to ease loneli-
ness, but he had never expected Harriet to use
him thus.

Harriet sat before a crackling fire in the drawing
room smiling at her gentlemen callers until her
face hurt. Lord Grafton had not appeared, much
to her relief and her father's questioning. But
George had not come either and that gave her
pause.

She had gone back to Tyre house with Sally
earlier that morning to search again for her missing pantalettes, only to return empty-handed and
scared to pieces. If someone had found them, it
was only a matter of time before it was broadcast
through the gossip columns. Would they guess
they were hers? With initials such as H.W., she
knew that they would indeed realize to whom
they belonged.

George would know if the news got out. He
had escorted her to find the privy, for heaven's
sake. He would put two and two together and
then what? He would know that she had lied to
him.

She had not meant to lie, but when faced with
the foolishness of her actions, she did not know
what to do. She certainly did not have time to
explain, and so she had let a terrible fib stand in
place of the truth.

When the last of her callers had gone, her
mother approached her with a soft touch to her
shoulder. "Harriet, are you feeling well dear? You
look a little pale."

"I am fine, Mother, just tired." She had not slept well and the dreary day dragged on for what seemed an eternity. And George had not called. Perhaps he merely had other business to attend to. The vision of the tiny blonde he had paid attention to last night flashed before her, causing still more concern. What if he chose to call upon *her* instead?

"Perhaps you should lie down," her mother said. "We are promised to dine at Lord and Lady Darwent's this evening."

Harriet had barely heard her mother, but she nodded and did as she was bid. Her thoughts would not give her rest as she lay on her bed. She chastised herself over and over for the poor example she had portrayed to George. Man's evil nature, she mused. She had certainly displayed some of that in strong measure and she was sorely ashamed. She closed her eyes, hoping George attended the same dinner this evening. She needed to find out what he had heard.

"Farley, something is wrong," his wife said as she swirled a fine shawl about her shoulders.

"What do you mean?"

"Mr. Clasby did not call today."

"Perhaps the scoundrel has gone off to find new prey," Lord Whitlow grumbled.

"That is not fair. Harriet has been fretting all day."

"You see, I told you this would happen, Prue." Lord Whitlow adjusted his cravat in the cheval mirror. "I knew he would bring heartache to our daughter if we let him near her."

His wife did not look the least bit convinced. "Harriet was not herself today, but she certainly did not appear heartbroken. Worried was more like it, but she would not talk to me which is most unusual."

"I hardly think she will talk to me," Lord Whitlow defended.

"Keep your ears open tonight, will you, dear?" his wife asked. "Perhaps we might find out what troubles her so."

He shrugged his shoulders but agreed, whatever good it would do. He had expected Lord Grafton to be among his daughter's callers this afternoon, especially after he had escorted Harriet to the Tyre Ball. The young man had not put in an appearance just as Clasby had not. The more he thought about it, the more odd it seemed.

Chapter Eleven

*T*he morning was dashed cool and mist rose
from the fields of lush green grass as George
waited for DeVillars' carriage. Freddie and Lord
Cherrington acted as his seconds. George realized
after it was too late that by asking Cherrington to
stand with him, Artemis would know and she
would no doubt tell Harriet.

Harriet!

How she haunted his thoughts. He envisioned
her slipping quickly into the Tyres' billiards room
at least a hundred times since DeVillars had
thrown her pantalettes at him. Why had she done
such a thing? Why had she risked her reputation?
And more importantly, why had she confessed to
forgetting to don undergarments when she had
obviously taken them off to leave behind for anyone to find?

"DeVillars." Freddie pointed toward the carriage making its way to Primrose Hill.

"Promise me you won't kill him," Lord Cherrington said with a lopsided grin. "Artemis will

never forgive me if I'm involved in any way with DeVillars' demise."

George answered with a rueful snort. "I am beginning to regret challenging the fool." Had he kept his temper in check, he would not be standing on the brink of ruining his efforts to restore his name. "But I do not plan to kill my irritating friend, as tempting as it may be."

DeVillars got out of his carriage and his two seconds followed close behind him. He looked pale and not a little remorseful for starting this farce.

"Good morning, Jory," George called out cheerfully. "Ready to meet your maker?" He was not about to let on that he would not put a bullet through the man's heart. It would serve him right to be scared silly after the damage he had caused. Gentlemen did not keep their mouths shut for long. The news of Harriet's undergarment as well as George's duel would no doubt be spread through the *ton* gossips soon enough.

"That is a question that should be asked of you, Clasby. So long have you questioned the existence of God, perhaps you will finally find out the truth of the matter when you lie dead upon the ground."

"I think I have come to know the truth," George said. "I only doubted because of worthless creatures such as yourself."

"And what has changed your mind?" DeVillars took off his coat.

"I recently heard a convincing argument that man's nature is naturally evil without God's influence. Our meeting this morning only supports such a theory, would you not agree?"

"That makes no sense." DeVillars stopped looking over the pistols and cocked his head to one side. "We were speaking of the existence of God, not evil."

"But you really cannot have one without the other," George pointed out.

DeVillars shook his head and resumed his inspection of his pistols.

George took off his own coat and threw it toward Freddie. Then he grabbed a pistol. "Are we ready to make our paces?"

"Indeed."

George and DeVillars squared off. Then they took twenty-seven paces each in opposite directions. The seconds were about to set the mark when another carriage careened into the field.

"The deuce," George uttered. "Who could that be?" He soon found out. A crested carriage belonging to Lord Whitlow pulled to a halt.

Whitlow stepped down wearing a fierce frown. "What the devil is going on here?" he raged.

"A duel, sir," Lord Cherrington offered.

"Blast and tarnation, I know that!" Lord Whitlow approached George. "Just what do you think you are doing?"

George's irritation grew. This man no longer intimidated him. He wanted a pompous simpleton like Grafton for his intelligent and sensitive daughter. Besides, George had just blown any chances he had for respectability. It no longer mattered what Whitlow thought of him. "I am defending your daughter's honor, my lord," George said in a sharp tone.

"So I have heard, but what I want to know is why? What have you done to her?"

"I have done nothing, but perhaps we might discuss this when we have finished." George was not about to be further delayed. He wanted the thing done. The longer they tarried, the more likely they were to get caught.

Lord Whitlow drew closer. "Don't you dare kill that boy," he whispered. "And if he doesn't kill you, I just might."

"I had not planned to," George answered just as quietly. "May we resume? You may have your turn after honor is served."

Given no choice, Lord Whitlow backed away and stood near Lord Cherrington, looking grim.

DeVillars and George squared off once again. Freddie read the rules and then DeVillars' second was given the honor of announcing the commencement of the duel.

George readied himself and turned just as DeVillars turned and shot. The bullet missed George completely and George threw off his aim enough that his bullet only nicked DeVillars' shoulder, throwing him to the ground.

"Do you feel vindicated?" DeVillars asked when George drew near.

"I do not, but this will have to do. Upon my honor and my word as a gentleman—which still has some merit—and in front of Miss Whitlow's father, I did not, nor did I ever intend to, dishonor Harriet Whitlow." He gave his friend a hand to help him up.

DeVillars bowed, giving the win to George. "Then perhaps you should find out what your respectable little vixen is up to leaving these lying about." DeVillars threw the offending pair of pantalettes at George. That went without saying, but being a loose-tongued fool, DeVillars had to state the obvious.

"I shall take your advice into consideration," George said as he picked up the scrap of linen from off of the grass. The two men bowed and nodded, as did their seconds, and then DeVillars left, taking Freddie with him.

Lord Whitlow looked as though his patience had run out. "What is this bloody well about?"

"How did you find out about this, my lord?" George asked calmly in the face of a building storm about to break. He did not mistake the slanted glance Whitlow gave Lord Cherrington, who climbed into the carriage to wait. Of course Artemis had sent word.

"Lady Cherrington asked that I make certain you did not get yourself killed. But I am not entirely convinced you should live to see the end of this day." Lord Whitlow looked more annoyed than angry.

"I am the better shot," George explained with a shrug of his shoulders. "I was in no real danger."

"After all that I had heard about you, I did not know you had experience with duels."

"Only once, really. DeVillars did not want a

blood bath," George said as a matter of fact. "He simply wished to get under my skin like the bugger he is."

Whitlow ignored his vulgar retort. "I demand to know what this has to do with Harriet."

George looked him straight in the eye. "DeVillars insulted Miss Whitlow. I reacted poorly, perhaps, but I could not let that rascal get away with insinuating . . ." George paused and searched for the right words. He was not about to repeat DeVillars' words to Whitlow. "Any dishonor to her person."

Whitlow narrowed his gaze and appeared to look through George.

"These were found at the Tyre ball." George handed over the lacy drawers. "DeVillars claims they belong to Harriet. I have never seen them before. Upon my word, I have not compromised her in any fashion." He was alone with her but they had not even kissed!

Shock registered across Whitlow's face and then his complexion took on an almost purple hue. He looked ready to explode. "How can these be hers?"

George felt his own anger simmering just below his calm exterior. "You must ask your daughter."

Lord Whitlow was going to do just that. He rode his carriage back to Mayfair, looking forward to solid answers as to why two men might duel over his Harriet! Mr. Clasby had not looked the least bit pleased with the situation nor did he wear any vestiges of guilt. He did not think the bounder lied either, to his complete relief. That left Harriet's explanation as the key to all of it. It was an explanation he very much wished to hear.

Harriet woke to sunshine streaming through her window. She stretched like a cat and threw back her coverlet. She sat up and stared a moment until she remembered her current situation with dread. Her pantalettes! She had to read the gossip column in the *Morning Post* and see if there was any mention of found undergarments.

She got out of bed and fetched her wrap. She looked at the lovely costume hanging on the outside door of her wardrobe. The long length made it necessary to hang it as high as possible to keep the train from the floor. The bright blue silk fabric was the color of a cloudless afternoon sky. She had a wig and accessories to complete her character perfectly. Tonight was the masquerade!

It was early and Sally had not yet brought in her chocolate or the newspaper, but Harriet did not wish to wait. She left her bedchamber and wandered down the hall. She would step into the kitchens and see if she could not gather up a small pot of chocolate for herself.

She could not possibly hope to return to sleep. She was wide-awake and brimming with nervous excitement and anxiety. Surely George would call today. If he did not, she would be beside herself with discouragement, but at least she would see him at the Ponsonby masquerade.

She passed the door to her parents' rooms and noticed a crumpled note upon the floor. She bent down and picked it up. She opened it to see if it was of any importance, and as she read, she felt as if the breath had been knocked out of her body.

Dear Lord Whitlow,
 My husband has left to second a duel between George Clasby and another. Cherry has described little, but I must warn you. I implore you to see what can be done to ensure Mr. Clasby's safety. For Harriet's sake, please intervene.
 Yours fearfully,
 A.
 Lady Cherrington.

Harriet shuddered. Cold with fear, she stood shivering in the hall, unsure of what to do. The clock below struck the hour of eight. Whatever had happened, it was too late for her to do anything. And her father had not yet returned.

The door to her parents' rooms opened.

"Harriet? What are you doing standing there like you have seen a ghost?"

Harriet felt her mother's warm arms wrap around her. Gratefully, she melted into her mother's embrace. "What am I to do?" Harriet whispered.

Her mother read the note. "Oh dear. Come with me. We shall have tea and a fire in the drawing room while we wait for your father to return."

Harriet paced the drawing room floor biting her already short nails. Her voluminous robe flared out as she took each turn. "Do you think he made it in time?" she asked her mother.

"I am certain that he has, dear. Now do not fret so. Come and drink your tea before it grows cold."

"But why? Why would George agree to a duel and with whom?" A vision of Lord Grafton's frowning face materialized in Harriet's mind and she nearly groaned aloud. What if Lord Grafton had challenged George to a duel? She would never forgive herself if either of them were hurt.

Surely not, she thought. She could not imagine Lord Grafton dueling. He did look angry enough after the Tyre ball but that fury had been solely directed toward herself, not George. But had she been mistaken?

"I do not know. We will simply have to wait."

Harriet stopped before the roaring fire that had been made up to warm her. It was of no use. She still shivered. They waited until the sound of the front door opening brought Harriet running out of the drawing room and down the hall to the entry.

"Is George all right?" she blurted, tears rolling down her face.

Her father gave her a rueful smile before he handed his top hat and gloves to their butler. "He is fine, Harriet, just fine."

Relief flooded through her, weakening her knees. Her father caught hold of her just before she stumbled to the floor. "Thank goodness," she breathed. "I have been worried this age."

"We must talk *now*," her father said with a stern voice she had rarely heard. He squeezed her shoulders comfortingly nonetheless.

She chewed her bottom lip, worry taking over where fear had just left off. "What is it?"

"Where is your mother?" he asked.

"Right here, dear," her mother called from the entrance of the drawing room.

"Let us go to my study, shall we?" Her father led the way.

Harriet exchanged a nervous glance with her mother and they both followed obediently, but Harriet did not relish the upcoming discussion. Something in her father's tone made it quite clear that she was deeply in the briars. She had heard this same voice used on several occasions with her brother. It did not bode well.

Once inside the study, her father shut the door. Despite the early hour of the day, he turned to his brandy, poured a small amount in a glass, and downed it with one gulp.

"Farley, whatever is it?" Her mother's eyes were wide.

Her father said nothing, but instead reached inside his coat and pulled out a neatly folded bit of white linen. He shook out the material to reveal a lacy pair of pantalettes. "Do these belong to you?"

Harriet thought she would be ill. Embarrassment like she had never felt before washed over her. Mortified, she reached out an unsteady hand and touched the fabric. Desperately she searched for a way to deny the truth, but her conscience got the better of her. She could not lie to her father. "They are mine."

Her father made a fist and pounded his desk, startling Harriet and her mother. "Would you explain how a rake named DeVillars got a hold of them?"

"DeVillars?" Harriet asked completely confused. "I do not even know a Mr. DeVillars."

"Yes, you do. He asked permission to pay his addresses your first Season. I sent him packing. He is a slippery fellow who is apparently a *friend* of your Mr. Clasby. I cannot say I like the company he keeps, but that is neither here nor there. Harriet, did George Clasby or, heaven help me, DeVillars, have anything to do with the removal of these?" His voice cracked when he held up the offending garment. Her father's neck was red and so were his cheeks, but the deep lines around his tightly pursed lips were white.

Harriet looked at her mother who waited for her answer with eyes revealing shock and disappointment. "They did not," Harriet choked out. "I removed them myself in an attempt . . ." She swallowed hard. Another moment and she would dissolve into tears.

"An attempt to what?" her father goaded.

Harriet shut her eyes tightly. "In an attempt to chase away Lord Grafton for good," she wailed.

"What the devil does he have to do with this?"

"Now, Farley," Harriet's mother said calmly. "Let the girl explain."

Harriet took a deep breath and wiped her tear-filled eyes. She had to get a modicum of control over herself. She was tempted to ask for a spot of brandy, but having never tasted the stuff before, she was afraid it would only make matters worse. "Lord Grafton was on the verge of proposing to me," she finally said.

"Of course he was. I gave him permission to do so," her father interrupted. A look from her mother silenced him.

"I will not marry him, not now, not ever," Harriet said with a stamp of her foot. It felt good to let her anguish have its way. Anger was far preferable to breaking into sobs. "I feared you might override my wishes of refusal, or worse, forbid me to see George. I had to prevent Lord Grafton from proposing. I had to do something to change his mind, make him loathe the very thought of offering for me."

Her father sat down behind his desk with a look of utter disbelief and confusion. He kept quiet, though.

"Do you know Lucinda Bronwell?" Harriet asked.

"Yes, but what does she have to do with—"

"Hear me out, Father, please," Harriet cut him off. "Last year she fell into the pond at the Collingtons' breakfast. She had not worn a chemise and her dress was quite transparent. Remembering Lucinda gave me the idea." Harriet feared she was not making a bit of sense, but she plundered on. "You see, Lord Grafton was repulsed by Lucinda's attempts to display her charms to him. I noticed that. I figured that if I were to appear with a clinging gown in front of him, he would also be repulsed by me and decide not to propose. And you see, it worked. I simply had not planned on just how well I would succeed."

"But how did Mr. DeVillars get a hold of your drawers?" her mother asked.

"I haven't the faintest idea. At the Tyre ball, I took them off and stuffed them behind a pillow in the billiards room. I had planned to retrieve them before I left, but Mr. Clasby noticed my uh"—she searched for the right words—"lack of discretion and immediately rushed to alert me. He offered to take me home to change." She looked at her parents, hoping they would understand the nobility of George's gesture. They did not appear impressed. She continued, "Lord Grafton decided that he should take me home and I forgot all about leaving my undergarments behind until it was too late. I sent Sally back for them, but they were already gone. I suppose DeVillars must have taken them."

Ashamed, Harriet slumped into a chair and bowed her head. She braced herself for their reactions. When none came, she peeked up at her father.

He looked as though he had received a stinging slap with a wet towel. "Young lady, this does not mean that I will allow you to marry a man like Clasby who, I might add, has just participated in his second duel!"

Harriet felt a lump thickening in her throat. She stood wondering if this was how criminals felt when they faced the gallows. "There is no chance of that now. You see," she choked out. "I lied.

Mortified by what I had done, I told him I had forgotten to wear my underthings." She could bear it no longer and cried, "He could have been killed because of my foolishness!"

She ran from the study, up the stairs, and into her bedchamber where she threw herself upon her bed and sobbed until she was spent.

Lord Whitlow remained seated at his desk. His wife walked behind him and rubbed his stiff shoulders.

"You should rethink your position toward Mr. Clasby, dear," she said.

"Never!"

"Really, he has done nothing so terrible."

"He is a rake and a scoundrel who challenged a man to a duel." He was not ready to concede to the inevitable. Not yet.

"Perhaps, but I think he loves our Harriet. He may not know that yet, but they both light up like fireflies when they look upon each other. Perhaps he felt bound by honor to defend Harriet. At least he did not stand idly by. He obviously took offense to this Mr. DeVillars just as any young man in love would do." She wrapped her arms around him and kissed his cheek. "And rightly so, it sounds like. Mr. Clasby fought for Harriet, like you once fought for me."

He sighed deeply. He supposed some of the blame must be laid at his own feet. Harriet had been afraid to refuse Grafton. He had all but insisted that she would marry the young lord. Had he trusted his daughter's own judgment a little more, perhaps she would not have felt compelled to go to the drastic length of ruining her reputation to keep Grafton from proposing to her.

"Wife," he finally said, "what are we to do now?"

"Let me talk to Harriet once she has settled down. We have a masquerade to attend this evening. I believe Mr. Clasby will be there. He and Harriet had planned to dress as characters from the book they are reading together. My advice is to let it be for now. Give the two of them the chance to work this through. Love will win out in the end."

Chapter Twelve

*H*arriet sat silently in the carriage with her parents as they made their way to Lord and Lady Ponsonby's annual masquerade. George had not called. She wondered if he ever would again.

"This will work itself out, dear, you shall see," her mother said softly. She had dressed in her usual Queen Elizabeth costume complete with pearls and pale face powder.

Harriet did not answer. She could not, since tears threatened to overcome her at any given moment. She squeezed her mother's hand and glanced at her father, who had dressed as Henry VIII.

Her father's frown suited his attire well. He looked ready to behead someone and not too particular as to whom. The situation was entirely her fault, but there were only so many apologies a daughter could utter without sounding trite.

She was indeed sorry for taking off her pantalettes. She had not only risked ruining her reputation but the Whitlow name would also suffer if it became known that Harriet had left her undergarments laying about after spending considerable time in George Clasby's presence.

Harriet had looked through this morning's edition of the *Post*, and nothing had been mentioned in the gossip column. But it was still early yet. The town tabbies would eventually know and it would no doubt be the main topic of conversation. Her last Season would indeed be miserably memorable, she thought.

They pulled into the line of carriages that stood waiting in the drive. They each put on their masks before stepping out into the night air, hoping to keep their identities secret until the unmasking hour of midnight.

Once inside the entrance hall of the huge Ponsonby town house, Harriet drifted apart from her parents. She did not wish to spoil their evening with her dour mood. Staying home had not been an option, even though Harriet did not feel the least bit like celebrating. She hoped to speak to George, but she could hardly go to his residence, and a letter would not do justice to the apology she owed him.

She searched the bevy of guests for a Knights Templar tunic, or even a black knight's armor, but she was sorely disappointed. There were cavaliers and pirates aplenty, but Harriet had not seen a single knight—in shining armor or otherwise.

She spotted a tall man with dark hair garbed in a somber black robe and realized it was Lord Grafton. As he approached, it dawned on her that he was dressed like the clergy of centuries past. She summoned her courage. "Good evening, Lord Grafton."

He looked at her curiously until recognition dawned and with it, complete distaste. "Miss Whitlow," he said with a curt nod. He did not stop to speak further with her but kept walking past. It was nearly the cut direct. She had hoped to beg his pardon, but clearly he wanted nothing from her.

She shrugged her shoulders and made her way to the refreshment table with a weary sigh. She supposed she deserved the dressing down she received from her parents. She even deserved George's anger, but she wished he was not ignoring her so.

"There are always consequences to one's actions," she said primly to herself. Had she not heard that sermon time and again from the curate at the Whitlow chapel? She could not put the desired end as justification for the means.

Remorse was very poor company for self-pity, and Harriet felt deeply sorry for herself. She had made a complete mull of things. If she would only have risen above her cowardice and voiced her opinions beforehand, perhaps she would not be in such a mess.

The refreshment table was laden with all manner of delicacies, but Harriet wanted nothing to eat. In fact, she had eaten little all day. She reached for a glass of lemonade and then decided against it when she saw the huge bowl of punch.

She dipped the ladle and filled an empty cup. She sipped it and then took a bigger gulp. The punch was good, spicy and sweet with a hint of rum.

She felt the warmth spread through her insides. After a few moments and another cupful, she did not feel quite so melancholy. Perhaps things were not as bleak as they seemed, she reasoned. She took another deep sip from her cup. Once she explained to George what had happened, surely he would understand. He had to.

"Have you seen Harriet?" Lady Whitlow asked.

Lord Whitlow turned at his wife's voice. "She is near the refreshment table with Lady Cherrington, I believe."

"She looks quite animated." His wife looked through to the ballroom. "I am certain she will be just fine."

"I suppose we will have to accept that jackanapes if he'll have her after all this," he grumbled. He did not like the idea that George Clasby was paramount to his daughter's happiness. But there it was, staring him in the face. Her tearful apologies had nearly torn his heart in two, but she had to face the music after what she had done.

"I see Grafton over there," he informed his wife. "I shall have a word with him and hopefully play a game of billiards to smooth over his ruffled feathers. If you need me, I shall be there."

"Do you not wish to dance, dear?" His wife smiled sweetly.

"Perhaps a little later."

"Very well. I shall be in the ladies' card room playing whist."

Lord Whitlow leaned forward to drop a kiss upon his lovely wife's white painted forehead. "Have a nice time, my dear. Do not wager too deep."

His wife cast him a look he knew well. She was in complete control of her pin money and would do exactly as she pleased.

George took the steps two at a time. He was late. As much as he was disappointed in Harriet's behavior, he still wanted to see her, talk to her, and try to understand her side of things. At the last minute, after this morning's adventure, he decided he must alter his costume. He had spent the better part of the afternoon visiting Bond Street and the theater district in order to make his desired revisions.

He walked into the Ponsonbys' grand ballroom and searched the elegantly dressed noblemen and women, the fairy queens and ruffians, until he finally saw her. Harriet stood near the refreshment table with a woebegone expression upon her sad little face as she contemplated her cup of punch.

She had dressed as the fair Saxon maid Rowena. She wore a long flaxen wig that made her look even more pale than usual. Her bright blue gown draped her slender figure nicely; the golden chain belt that hung about her hips accentuated the delicate curve of her body.

Harriet looked up and caught him admiring her,

and her eyes widened behind the silly little mask she wore. She had indeed recognized him but her smile was forced and unsure.

George's anger melted away.

"Miss Whitlow." He bowed when he finally reached her. "You do the fair Rowena justice."

"Thank you, George," she said almost sleepily. "And what a wonderful knight you make."

"Don't you recognize who I am supposed to be?" he asked.

She looked him up, then back down, and smiled broadly. "Ivanhoe?"

"Of course, Ivanhoe!" He had gone to considerable trouble to find a long mail tunic and a leather jerkin. He carried a shield with a crest and a sword in the scabbard that was fastened around his waist. His head was covered with tiny chain links of mail that pulled at his hair when he moved his head too fast. He even wore a helmet that covered most of his face.

He held out his arm. "Would you care to dance?" The soft strains of a waltz started.

"Yes, sir knight." She bowed low and would have toppled over had he not reached out to steady her.

"Are you all right?" he asked.

"Now that you are finally here and speaking to me, I do believe I am." Her words were slightly slurred.

George leaned close to her mouth and sniffed. "How much punch have you had?" he asked.

"Don't know, don't care," she smiled fully at him.

"Devil a bit," he muttered. He carefully led her onto the dance floor, grateful the dance was a waltz so that he could keep her close against him. "Harriet, you are foxed," he whispered more to himself than her, since Harriet did not appear to be listening. She was humming along to the music.

"Have you danced with anyone else?" he asked. She was bound and determined to ruin herself and he did not understand why.

"Only you," she said. "It has always been and always will be only you." Then she took great interest in the head covering he wore. "I have always liked the color of your hair," she said a little too loudly. "It is too bad you have covered it up."

Embarrassment washed over him when he realized the couple dancing next to them had overheard her remark. "Yes, well." He had to do something fast, before more scandal was brought down around their ears in the middle of the Ponsonby ballroom.

He searched the vast room for Harriet's parents. But of course, he had no idea how they were dressed. And he could hardly allow Lord Whitlow to discover his daughter's state, else the blame for her overindulgence in rum punch would no doubt be laid at his feet.

"George," Harriet murmured. "Do you remember the Christmas kiss we shared at Rothwell Park?"

He pulled her closer to keep her moving, but her steps faltered and slowed. "Yes." He saw a tall couple waltzing gracefully near the balcony and knew in an instant what must be done. He maneuvered an indecently close Harriet toward them.

"Did you like it?" She focused on his mouth and licked her lips.

He felt a surge of panic. What if she tried to kiss him here? Another turn and he was nearly beside Lady Cherrington, dressed as her namesake, Artemis—Goddess of the Hunt. "Lady Cherrington," he hissed.

She turned and smiled. "Mr. Clasby?" she asked.

"Yes, 'tis I."

"I'm so relieved you have come." Her expression turned to one of concern when she noticed Harriet trying to take off his helmet.

He jerked his head away. "She has had too much punch."

"Oh dear." She looked up at her husband, who grinned as if the whole thing were amusing. "I knew I should not have left her alone. She was in such a brown study."

"I need to get her out of here before she does something regrettable." George felt his face flame when Harriet nuzzled into his neck.

"What can we do to help?" Lord Cherrington asked.

"Oh hullo, Cherry," Harriet slurred. "George has not answered whether he liked my kiss."

"Miss Whitlow, what are you about?" Lord Cherrington said softly as his wife looked on with worry.

"About? I am about to capture George once and

for all," Harriet said, and then her head drifted to his shoulder.

George exchanged an exasperated look with the Cherringtons. "I shall do my best to sober Miss Whitlow and return as soon as possible. My town house is just around the corner. My housekeeper, Mrs. Sweet, will help." He wanted them to know he and Harriet would be chaperoned at all times.

"Should we come with you?" Artemis asked.

"No. Keep an eye on her parents, if you please. They cannot see her this way. After this morning, it would only make matters more difficult for her father." He did not need Lord Whitlow thinking any worse of him than he already did, nor did he need to make another trip to Primrose Hill.

"We understand." Cherrington turned about with his wife. "Go quickly through the gardens. Less chance of anyone seeing you."

George did not waste another moment. He shifted Harriet to wake her and then turned and dipped them toward the opened door leading to the terrace. "Come now, Harriet, let's hurry."

"Where are we going?" she said sleepily.

"We need to walk a bit." He pulled her along. The cool night air seemed to have a positive effect on her drowsiness. "We need to hurry, my dear," he said.

They dashed through the gardens and crossed the lawns of a few homes and turned north toward his town house. Taking care to remain in the shadows and courtyards not fenced off from the public, they nearly ran.

She tripped and fell to her knees in the soft grass, letting out a broken sob.

"Harriet," he whispered, alarmed. "What is it? Are you hurt?"

"I am so terribly sorry about the duel," she wailed. "I never meant for that to happen. Oh how you must hate me!"

He knelt down next to her and took off his cursed helmet. "I do not hate you," he said. *I was mad as a hornet,* he thought. "I could never hate you. Come now, Harriet, get up. We must hurry."

She sat back upon her feet instead. Her tears continued in streams down her face. "I was so worried. You did not call yesterday nor did you come this afternoon, and then it was ages before you arrived tonight." She gathered the silken material of her dress around her knees as she stared searchingly up at him. "I thought you were not going to come at all, and I feared you never wanted to speak to me again." She ended with a hiccup.

"Harriet." He knelt closer. A large teardrop lay on the tip of her eyelash and glistened in the glow of the nearby gaslight. He reached out and wiped it away with his fingertip. "Please do not cry."

"I have tried so very hard to make you love me. I fear I have done the very opposite instead." She grabbed hold of his hands.

George froze. *Love?*

"I have loved you," Harriet said in a low voice that was barely above a whisper, "from the first time you spoke to me at my come-out."

Warmth spread through his body and he tightened his hold on her hands. Was it true? Or were the multiple glasses of rum punch she had swallowed talking to him instead?

Harriet looked down at their clasped hands. "I have been too much of a coward to tell you." And then she looked deeply into his eyes. "George? Please say something."

"Harriet—" He was cut off when she threw her arms about his neck and kissed him.

Harriet had reached her wits' end. George had been staring at her as if she had just turned into a turnip. She pulled his face to hers and planted her lips firmly upon his. He knelt beside her, frozen as if he was unsure what to do. But Harriet showed him what she wanted.

She moved her lips softly against his until she felt his arms tighten around her, pulling her close. She could feel the rough leather jerkin he wore through the thin silk of her gown and pulled him even closer. Then she surrendered to the heady experience of being conquered by a most worthy knight.

She opened her mouth, realizing that was what George wanted her to do. She was immediately glad that she did. His tongue touched hers and twined around in an intimate dance that set her aflame with desire.

She moaned and tilted her head back when his hands dragged the wig off of her head. His lips left hers only to kiss a heated trail along her jaw as his fingers threaded through her fine hair. She opened her eyes to stare at the stars above, reveling in the feel of George's lips upon her skin. His mouth traveled lower along her neck until she became dizzy and sprawled backwards onto the ground, pulling him down with her.

"Harriet," he groaned. He kissed her exposed skin just above the modest neckline, sending a delicious shiver down her spine. "We must stop." He nuzzled her ear.

Somewhere inside her rum-fuzzy head she knew he was correct, or else they would plunder into sheer folly. But now that she had him just where she wanted him, she did not wish to let go. "We could go to Gretna Greene," she whispered.

George stopped as if he had just been drenched with a bucket of cold water. He pulled back and sat up quickly. "No, no, we definitely cannot do such a thing." He stood, then bent down to help her to her feet.

"Why not?" The ground swirled beneath her slippers and she reeled toward him, her head pounding in her ears.

George steadied her. "Because my reputation would not bear it, nor would yours."

"Reputation!" Harriet pulled her hand away. "I know the only reason you sought me out was to heal your wounded reputation. Do those kisses mean nothing then?"

"I shamefully admit that I did seek to call on you with the hope that I could restore my good name. Harriet, I loathe to confess that."

She placed a shaking hand to her head. "Then do not. What difference does it make now? After news travels about the reason for your duel, my name will have sunk beneath contempt. I am as good as ruined once word gets out."

"It is because of those kisses we shared that I would never whisk you off to Gretna. It would only make matters worse. Your father would never forgive us. 'Tis not right to put him through that kind of worry."

Harriet knew he was indeed correct, but it did not matter any longer. She wanted to marry him and she realized that she was old enough to do so without her parents' permission. But she so desperately wanted their approval.

Her stomach turned over and she tried to make sense of what George said and the thoughts running rampant inside her brain. She feared she did not feel well at all and trembled with a horrible chill.

"Do you not see?" said George. "I wish to have the ability to wed the most decent and well-respected lady in town. That would hardly happen if we were to traipse to Gretna." His smile was tender and he chuckled lightly.

Harriet did not like the sound of his excuse, but with her belly roiling, she could not think clearly enough to know he spoke about her. "George," she gasped. "I do not feel well."

"Come along, Harriet." He stretched out his hand toward her. "We have some repairing to do in order to make it back to the party before midnight. My housekeeper will make coffee, and in no time you will be back to normal."

The thought of coffee and its pungent smell

made her feel that much worse. She could hold on no longer. She dropped back down to her knees and heaved, casting up every drop of rum punch she had swallowed.

It was horrible. Harriet wished the earth would open up and gobble her into oblivion. George knelt next to her. He rubbed her back and purred soothing words into her ear, like one would do for a sick infant. Her eyes blurred with tears and she coughed. And then she started to shiver and shake. "This is terrible," she whispered, her teeth chattering.

"Yes, it is," George agreed with a chuckle.

She leaned back on her haunches and took the handkerchief George offered to wipe her mouth. She would not look at him. Her head pounded, and all she wanted to do was lay down and close her eyes in hopes that the ground would stop spinning.

"Do you think you can stand?" George asked.

"I think I would like to die," Harriet said with a groan.

"You will feel better soon, I promise." George wrapped his arm around her shoulders and helped her to stand. "Come on. My town house is very close."

Harriet did not say a word. She walked into George's embrace wondering what had happened to her levelheaded demeanor. She had sunk beneath reproach. She remembered confessing to George that she loved him and that filled her with even more regret. What he must think of her!

Chapter Thirteen

George helped Harriet up the steps to his town house as Mrs. Sweet stepped forward. "Is everything all right, sir?"

"Coffee, Mrs. Sweet. Lots of hot strong coffee." George rubbed Harriet's arms briskly in an attempt to warm her. She had not stopped shaking since casting up her accounts. "Come into the kitchen where it is warm."

George kept his arm firmly around her, even though she still would not look at him. In the kitchen, Mrs. Sweet bustled about making the coffee. He pulled out a chair for Harriet and placed it close to the grate. A small but bright fire crackled and hissed, chasing away the night's chill.

"Harriet," he said softly. "There's no need for you to hang your head. Rum has that effect on many. And I will wager tonight's punch was stronger than most."

Harriet merely nodded.

Mrs. Sweet approached him with a warm shawl

in her hands. "I thought the lady could use this." She bowed, then returned to her task.

"Thank you." George said as he tenderly wrapped the shawl around Harriet's still-shaking shoulders. He brushed her cheek with his fingertips and conflicting emotions flooded through him. He wanted to wrap his arms around her and kiss the worry from her brow but he also wanted to shake her for placing them in this precarious situation.

"I have never felt so ashamed in my life," she muttered. "Once again, I have acted like a fool."

George could not help but chuckle. "What causes your distress, being three sheets to the wind or shooting the cat afterward?"

"I am so terribly happy that you find it amusing." She cast him a scathing look. "I have become a troublesome embarrassment to my parents, and I have done things only an insane person would do all because I am too much of a coward to speak my own mind."

"And did you speak your mind this evening?" he asked softly, hoping that she meant it when she said she loved him. But she did not hear him and continued in her self-deprecating tirade.

"I have more hair than wit and that is very little indeed." She pulled the shawl closer and sank deeper into the chair.

"Harriet, it is not so awful, really. We left well before anyone noticed your condition, except for Lord and Lady Cherrington, but they will tell no one."

"What about my parents? They will soon realize I am missing?"

"Lady Cherrington will take care of them. I asked that she keep her eyes upon your parents and do whatever is needed. Do not worry. We will be back in a trice with no one the wiser."

"But I am worried. The *ton* is bound to find out about the duel." She looked away from meeting his eyes.

He pulled a chair close to her and took her cold hands in his. "DeVillars had it coming. He knows it and so do the gentlemen who were present when I called him out."

She looked at him with harried concern. "But my pantalettes! What about those? When word gets out about those, I will be ruined."

"I have been wondering about that." George gently squeezed her hands. "What the devil were you trying to do?"

She pulled away from him and held her head in her hands, grasping her hair and groaning. "I was trying to prevent Grafton from proposing by squelching his admiration of my sterling character," she said sarcastically. "I had no idea I would look *that* transparent. I did not intend to leave my undergarments behind. I had planned to fetch them before I left, but I forgot completely when I realized how terribly scandalous I appeared. Lord Grafton was furious. Never will I forget his look of disgust."

"Grafton is a fool," George grumbled. He remembered the lovely shape of her legs seen clearly through the fabric of her skirt. Then he thought better of dwelling upon that vision. Perhaps it was not the wisest course of action with the subject of his lustful thoughts sitting in his kitchen.

He cleared his throat and asked another question that had been bothering him. "Why did you ask me to escort you to the water closet? You could have easily gone alone."

Harriet blushed. "I could no longer stand by and watch you—that is to say, you were bowing and scraping over the hand of that tiny blonde until I felt quite nauseated!"

"Miss Lawler?" He nearly hooted. She was jealous! He was more warmed by her reaction of envy than he imagined possible.

"Yes, *her*, Miss Lawler." Harriet flicked back a stray tendril of hair that fell before her eyes. "I decided there and then that if Grafton saw me leave with you . . ." She could not verbalize whatever she had wanted Grafton to think. "I wanted to use your reputation with the ladies to my advantage just as you have used my reputation to yours," she said in a rush.

Just then Mrs. Sweet set a tray before them. Silently, she poured steaming coffee into two cups.

"Black, I think," George said when Mrs. Sweet reached for the cream and sugar. Harriet scowled at him.

Mrs. Sweet tried to hide the smile that hovered on her lips as she handed a cup to Harriet, but it was quite clear that the housekeeper had enjoyed their entire conversation.

"Thank you," Harriet said shyly as if just realizing that they were not alone.

"Perhaps you should stay, Mrs. Sweet," George

said quickly when his housekeeper turned to leave.

Mrs. Sweet stepped closer. "Excuse me, sir, but the lady's gown is soiled. Would you like me to see what can be done?"

George had not noticed the grass stains on the front of Harriet's dress. That would cause yet another delay in returning to the masquerade, but it could not be helped. She could hardly return in her current state. "Is that agreeable to you, Miss Whitlow?" George asked.

Harriet nodded.

"Come, Miss Whitlow," Mrs. Sweet said softly. "You can change out of that gown in my rooms."

George watched Harriet disappear with his housekeeper and then he waited. It was indeed wise to keep Mrs. Sweet close by to play chaperone since he did not quite trust himself alone with Harriet. The feelings that coursed through him were new and strong. He felt a little drunk himself on the headiness of them.

Kissing her had been heaven on earth but he knew that if he tried to repeat the performance, they would indeed stray into dangerous territory. He smiled as he remembered how Harriet had approached him at Rothwell Park under the mistletoe. He smiled when he considered just how long had she wished to kiss him.

He turned when he heard soft footsteps. Harriet wore a dressing gown that belonged to Mrs. Sweet. It was white cotton with pink bows and much too big for Harriet, as the sleeves bunched around her wrists after being rolled several times.

Even disheveled and clothed in such an oversized wrap, Harriet looked lovely. Her soft brown hair hung down past her shoulders and it shone with streaks of gold in the fire's light.

"Please stop looking at me like that," Harriet whispered. She refilled her cup with steaming coffee and sat down.

"You truly are beautiful," he said, feeling awkward. They were completely alone since Mrs. Sweet worked on Harriet's costume in the laundry.

"But you have been linked with so many women much more taking than I."

"None of them compare to you," George said. "You are a mix of riddles, Miss Whitlow. And I find it exhilarating. You can deliver a convincing sermon and yet you are human enough to overindulge in rum punch when you are blue-deviled. I can honestly say that because of you, I want none of the life I once led."

She took another sip of her coffee and looked him straight in the eye. "What is it you want now then?"

George stilled his racing heart. He wanted her! He wanted a lifetime spent with her to discover the meaning of life. He would offer for her hand this very moment, but he needed to do the thing properly and that meant first speaking to her father, who all but despised him.

He set his cup of coffee aside. Time was fleeting and they had to return to the masquerade. "Harriet," he said as he stood. "Let me see if Mrs. Sweet has finished with your costume. What I want right now is to return before we are truly missed."

Her eyes widened and in them he read disappointment. He had not said what she wanted to hear. But he would, soon enough. Her rainy gray eyes clouded over, as if a storm waged inside of her. "George," she said quickly. "I humbly beg your pardon for creating so much trouble. If something had happened to you this morning. . . ."

He placed his finger upon her lips. "Do not think on it. Nothing happened and all will work itself out in the end."

Harriet gave him the faintest of smiles. "My mother said the very same thing earlier this evening."

"Your mother is a wise woman." He was anxious to get back. He wanted to speak with Lord Whitlow straightaway now that his mind had been made. He glimpsed a smiling Mrs. Sweet carrying Harriet's gown in her arms.

"I did the best I could, and I think I got most of it out. The spots will dry in no time," the housekeeper said.

He reached out his hand to Harriet. "I'll leave you with Mrs. Sweet to change."

Harriet downed the rest of her coffee and looked around. "My wig—where is it?"

George groaned. "I fear we left it somewhere on the way here."

"We must find it." She looked at him. "And your helmet?"

"No doubt lying by your wig."

*   *   *

Harriet held on tightly to George's strong hand as they dashed back the way they had come in search of the misplaced pieces of their costumes. She blushed at the memory of kissing him so boldly but she was not in the least sorry about doing so. George's kisses were pure magic and she longed to experience them again.

Even though she had been humiliatingly ill afterward, George had shown nothing but kindness toward her. She made an oath that she would stay clear of anything stronger than wine. But if she ever found herself in similar circumstances, she wanted George by her side.

She had landed in the briars each time she imbibed stronger spirits than she was used to, but through it all, she had found her source of courage. She vowed to become more outspoken and reveal her true desires. She simply could not keep them locked inside any longer.

The fact that George seemed to understand why she had done what she had gave her great hope. It would work out just as he said it would. It had to.

She believed that George might have been on the verge of declaring himself in his kitchen. And she hoped the reason he had not asked for her hand was that he wished to speak to her father. If she had somehow misread his intentions, she was still determined to do what she could to make the way clear to marry him.

She too would have a talk with her father and if he refused their union, she made a silent promise that she would indeed run to Gretna Green even if it meant kidnapping George to get him there.

She smiled at *that* thought.

"Feeling better?" he asked.

Indeed she was. She had made poor choices but at least she had taken control over the course of events. In time, she would improve how she handled various situations. "Thank you for taking care of me," she said softly.

George stopped and faced her. "It is my pleasure." He looked very earnest and noble. "In fact, I like taking care of you very much."

Harriet thought he made the perfect knight. With the mail hood thrown back, his hair curled in unruly auburn waves. She had always wanted to run her fingers through the thickness of his hair, but she hesitated. She had put him through the hatches tonight and they could not afford to dally. They needed to hurry back.

"You are an honorable knight." She brushed her fingers through his hair anyway, not wanting to lose this moment with him. "What made you choose to dress as Ivanhoe?"

He captured her hand, turned it over, and placed a light kiss upon her palm. "I planned to be a Knight Templar. I liked their tunics, don't you know. But after this morning, I thought Ivanhoe to be more appropriate."

She laughed. "Of course." And then the flaxen wig caught her attention and she pulled her hand away to point. "There is my wig! And your helmet."

"Thank goodness." George picked up both.

"My fair Rowena, if we tarry too long, we will face a heap of trouble."

"You are indeed correct." Harriet knew they were in store for a stern lecture from her father at the very least, but she feared it would be much more than that. For once, she felt ready to do battle.

They entered the Ponsonbys' estate through the terrace doors just minutes before the clock stuck midnight. They stepped into the ballroom carefully, hoping to slip in without calling attention to themselves and they nearly ran straight into Lord Whitlow's broad chest. He stood next to Lord Grafton.

"Clasby, Harriet," Whitlow blustered. "Where have you been? We have searched for you this past half hour or more."

George experienced a moment of brief relief. Whitlow had been searching for them for less than an hour, so he had no idea just how long they had been gone.

"Well?" Whitlow demanded.

"We were walking," Harriet said quickly.

It was the truth, just not quite all of it.

Her father reached out and pulled a bit of grass from Harriet's flaxen wig and his face turned red. Grafton looked shocked and glared accusingly at them both.

George's temper flared white-hot. "I had grass this morning before breakfast, I'll not hesitate to repeat the actions again if you do not wipe the filthy thoughts out of your head." George stepped toward Grafton.

When the pompous lord said nothing, only raised his brow with irritating arrogance, George puffed up his chest—ready to strike him with the back of his hand. "Name your—"

Harriet quickly stepped between them. "Please, George, no more dueling." She cast a glance toward her father for help.

"Indeed," Lord Whitlow said. "Harriet, find your mother. She is worried. Clasby, I think you have some explaining to do."

"Very well," George said. He waited for Harriet to leave. She took hold of his hand and squeezed quickly before staring down both her father and Lord Grafton. Then she went in search of her mother with her head held high.

George watched the gentle sway of her hips in the medieval-styled gown that she wore and sighed with pride. With blinding clarity, he realized he loved her. He felt as if a candle had been lit within the darkness of his heart and finally, he could see.

"Lord Whitlow." George felt light-headed with the knowledge of how strong was his love for Harriet. "I must inform you that I will have your daughter's hand in marriage with or without your blessings. But I greatly wish for your approval."

Lord Whitlow looked taken aback that he would make such a declaration in front of Lord Grafton.

Grafton coughed. He looked completely uncomfortable.

"And Grafton," George started, "you may as well forget any ideas you might have of offering for her. Harriet Whitlow is already spoken for." It felt good to rub that into the pompous lord's face.

Grafton narrowed his gaze as if measuring him. "I do believe you deserve each other." Then, surprisingly and without condescension, he added, "I bid you both good fortune." And then he bowed and walked away.

"Well, young man," Lord Whitlow said with a heavy sigh. "Do you wish to air our conversation in front of the whole *ton,* or can we speak privately?"

George inclined his head. He could have shouted his adoration for Harriet Whitlow from the middle of the room, but instead, he gestured for Whitlow to lead the way. "After you, my lord."

Lord Whitlow mumbled something that sounded very close to *insolent jackaknapes,* but George could not be sure. Even so, he followed his future father-in-law into a private room.

Harriet paced impatiently near the refreshment table. She had taken one look at the punch and her stomach rebelled with a lurching turn. She settled for a glass of lemonade instead and, amidst the strokes of midnight, told her mother everything that had transpired.

"Do you not see, George saved me from ruin once again," she said with more melodrama than was needed. "Surely you see how worthy he is, Mama."

"Yes, dear, but he could have come and found me," her mother pointed out.

"He could not have done so without Father blaming him for filling me full of rum punch. Which, again, was none of his doing." Harriet sat down with a groan. "What is taking them so long?"

"I do not know."

Several moments later, the two men stood before them. The surrounding guests unmasked with raucous laughter. George looked a little harried and the tops of his ears were red but otherwise no worse for wear.

"Well?" Harriet said.

"We shall talk more tomorrow morning," her father said. "Come, I think it is time that we leave. I find I am quite weary and I think I have aged twenty years in the last twelve hours!"

"But," Harriet said to the backs of her parents. She looked at George, who gave her a wink.

"I will see you tomorrow," he whispered. He looked at her with an encouraging nod and then he blew her a kiss. Harriet felt relieved and considerably hopeful.

Lord Whitlow pulled the covers back and slid gratefully into bed. He was exhausted. After making amends to Lord Grafton and hoping past hope that there might remain a chance for the boy, Harriet had come up missing with Clasby.

Lord and Lady Cherrington had done their best to stall, but he had seen through the charade. Harriet had been with George and neither of them was in the building. He had made a quick tour of the gardens with no sign of his daughter.

"Are you going to tell me what happened?" his wife asked as she settled in next to him. "You are too cruel to keep Harriet in the dark, anxiously awaiting your decision."

"It will serve her right to worry just a little. She has acted inappropriately and has brought whispers of scandal upon our name."

"It is her last Season, dear. She was desperate."

"Even so." He shrugged his shoulders. "She could have talked to me."

"I do not think you would have listened. The way you acted, you would have married Grafton yourself," his wife said with a playful pinch.

"He is a good man, Prue."

"Oh pooh, he is by far too stuffy for Harriet and you know it."

"Aye, perhaps you have the right of it."

"Of course I do, dear. Now tell me, did George ask to marry Harriet or not?"

"He didn't ask."

Suddenly furious, his wife sat straight up in bed.

Lord Whitlow chuckled and gestured for her to calm down. "The insolent charlatan *told* me that he would marry our Harriet with or without my blessings."

"Well, good for George," his wife murmured.

"Now see here," he blustered.

"He loves her."

"Aye, that he does."

"They shared only kisses, you know." His wife had cuddled back into his arms.

"That is what he assured me. But still, Harriet had grass in her wig!"

"My dear, Harriet was quite ill from too much rum punch and she did not have the luxury of a chamber pot. It is a wonder that there was *only* grass in her wig."

Lord Whitlow burst out laughing. "I cannot think of a sight more dampening to a man's amorous overtures. Thank the good Lord for the effects of rum punch!"

Chapter Fourteen

The next morning, Harriet knocked lightly upon the door leading to her father's study. She knew it was quite early, but she had a feeling her father might already be at work, hopefully planning out her marriage portion.

"Come in." Her father sounded like he was in good spirits.

She pushed open the door. "Papa, may I speak with you a moment?"

"Why, you are up early. Of course dear, come in, come in." He gestured with his hands for her to sit down.

She squared her shoulders and took the seat in front of the huge oak desk that dominated the room. "I owe you a heartfelt apology, Papa."

"Come now, Harriet, you have already done that." He gave her a slight smile. "Over and over, I might add."

"Yes, for the pantalettes and for the duel, but I should have trusted you enough to tell you exactly how I felt about George, I mean, Mr. Clasby."

Her father smiled. "I know, child. I too must humbly beg your pardon for trying to force you into marriage with a man you could never love."

"I so wanted to make you proud." Harriet's voice trembled with emotion.

Her father was up from behind his desk in a trice and pulling her into a warm embrace. "I am so very proud of you, my daughter. You have never once wavered from your course. Like your mother tried to pound into my stubborn head, you know your own heart. Now, now, do not cry, child. I cannot bear it."

"I love you, Papa," Harriet whispered. Tears rolled down her cheeks but they were tears of joy, not sorrow. She was indeed blessed with a wonderful father who had always wanted only the best for her.

"And I love you." He gave her a squeeze before letting go. "I suppose I shall have to get used to the idea that you are truly all grown up."

Harriet smiled. "Yes."

"And soon to be a married lady, no less," her father added with a wink.

Harriet threw her arms around her father once again. "Does that mean you have given George and me your full blessing?"

"Had to," her father answered and then let out a bark of laughter. "Your young man would accept no other answer. Now come, let us have something to eat. We cannot have you fainting away while Clasby does the pretty."

Harriet looped her arm through her father's. "Then let us eat because after last night, I find I am very hungry indeed."

Harriet sat demurely in the drawing room, waiting. She had bathed, donned her finest morning dress, and had Sally style her hair into a soft knot with a matching ribbon. Nothing could be done about the dark circles beneath her eyes, since she had hardly slept a wink the previous night. Her tossing and turning had been in anticipation of today. She glanced at the clock hanging upon the wall. It was only half past nine.

" 'Tis early, Harriet," her mother said. "Mr. Clasby may still be asleep."

Harriet hoped not. She could hardly sit still, and if she had to wait very much longer, she would send a footman to see what was keeping him. She looked at the clock again—thirty-five minutes past nine o'clock. Oh, where was he?

A sound in the hall brought Harriet out of her seat to check. It was George! She watched him give their butler his top hat and gloves, and then she quickly returned to her chair before he caught her spying. Her heart raced and she could not keep the smile from her face.

"Is it him?" her mother whispered.

"Yes." Harriet fluffed the skirt of her gown and quickly pinched her cheeks.

"Stop that," her mother admonished. "You look lovely."

"Mr. Clasby to see Miss Harriet," the butler announced.

Harriet looked up just as George walked into the room. Her insides fluttered and she felt warm and cold at the same time. He looked incredibly handsome in a dark blue superfine coat that hugged his shoulders without a crease. She stood and felt curiously light-headed, but not in the least dizzy. She was grateful that her father had suggested she eat a hearty breakfast, otherwise she might have swooned.

"Good day." Her voice was barely a whisper.

"Miss Whitlow," he said formally and then bowed to her mother. "Lady Whitlow." He stood quietly, almost awkwardly, without saying a word. Then he coughed. "I was wondering if I might, that is to say," his voice trailed off and he looked at Harriet for help.

Goodness, she thought. He acted terribly nervous. She licked her dry lips, sudden fear clutching her soul. She hoped he had not changed his mind.

"Let me give the two of you some privacy." Her mother smiled as she left the room, leaving the door open just a crack.

Harriet and George both watched her leave.

"George?" Harriet walked toward him. "Is everything all right?"

He pulled at his cravat. "I think so," he muttered.

"Then what is amiss? You seem a jumble of nerves."

"That is because I am," he said.

She reached for his hands, taking both into her own. "Why? Have you reconsidered calling upon me?" She could hardly ask if he no longer wished to wed her because he had not even asked her yet.

He blew out a deep breath. "Harriet," he started, then muttered, "devil a bit! I'm not doing this very well, am I?"

Harriet tensed. "What are you trying to do?" She hoped she was not wrong. Surely he had not changed his mind overnight. Her father had told her expressly that George wished to offer for her hand. Were they both mistaken?

"Might we sit down?" George said.

"Of course." They sat upon the settee. Harriet waited for what seemed like hours and still George had not spoken. Now she was truly frightened. If he did not want her after all, she might break down into a fit of hysterics and that would surely send George running for his hat and gloves.

George took her hands once again. His palms were damp. "Harriet," he said. "I beg your pardon, this is not easy."

"What, what is so difficult?" Harriet's heart pounded so hard in her chest it echoed in her ears.

"Asking you to marry me!"

Harriet blinked.

"Forgive me," he said. "Let me start over."

Harriet did not wait another moment. "Yes," she said.

"Yes what?" He looked almost confused.

Harriet thought he looked adorably flustered. "Yes, I will marry you," she said calmly even though her heart continued to beat hard, but this time with sheer joy.

"But I haven't asked you yet!"

"Well get on with it, will you?" Harriet said. "My parents are waiting."

He cocked his head as if annoyed. "Harriet, you are supposed to wait until you are properly asked. Must you always make a sham of a proposal?" His cheeks twitched and the hint of a smile hovered around his mouth. "I begin to feel sorry for Grafton. Cherrington told me what you put the poor man through."

Harriet lifted a pillow and hit him upon the head. "You had me worried to death!"

He reached after the pillow, but she held it high above her head, out of his reach. George leaned close and encircled her waist, pulling her against him. There was nothing for Harriet to do but drape her arms about his neck. She let the pillow drop and roll upon the floor, forgotten at their feet.

"I had an entire speech planned," he said. "And you have ruined it."

"I do not need a speech," she whispered.

"No? Then just what does the lovely Miss Whitlow need?" His breath was warm and sweet upon her face.

Harriet looked deeply into his eyes—their copper-colored irises had turned to fire. She said, "I need you to love me."

He brushed his lips softly against hers until she sighed. "I do love you, Harriet. It rather took me by surprise to realize just how much I adore you."

"I love you too, George. I have loved you from the moment I first saw you."

He smiled. "Well I will love you for always and

forever," he whispered before he kissed her in earnest.

Lord Whitlow stepped out of his study to spy his wife peeking through the drawing room door. He softly came up behind her. "Is he in there?"

"Yes, and nervous as a schoolboy. Farley, I fear poor George is frightened to pieces."

Lord Whitlow chuckled softly and then he peeked in as well. After George's insolence, he could hardly believe the boy had trouble proposing. But then, Clasby had admitted to never coming close to asking any young lady before.

"Ah, there, he has finally said it," his wife whispered with a giggle.

"Shouted more like," he muttered as he pulled at his wife's arm. "Come away, Prue. Give them their time. We have an announcement to make and we must arrange for a parish license and for the banns to be read."

His wife followed him back into his study. "What, no special license?"

"After news of the duel breaks out, I hardly think a special license wise." Lord Whitlow said. "The gossips will have enough to chatter about without adding a hasty wedding atop of it all. It will look as if they *had* to marry."

"If you insist dear, but I do not think we should make them wait. As it is, we can easily count off nine months with a special license."

He looked at his wife and realized the truth of her words. He was in no mood to watch over a pair of lovebirds like a hawk for the next month or more. It would send him to an early grave. "Very well. Let us apply to the archbishop of Canterbury, then."

His wife promptly kissed him on the cheek. "I shall begin arrangements for a ball."

Lord Whitlow merely shook his head. He had only one daughter and he was bound and determined to do whatever necessary to make his little mite happy.

Epilogue

George stripped off his shirt and breeches and threw them into the corner. "Harriet, do you wish to give it a try?"

His wife of nearly two months entered the tiled room he had reserved for the bath. "Do you think it will work?" she asked with a gleam in her eye.

"We shall simply have to find out, won't we?" He grinned. He loved the way his wife looked at him. He would never tire of the desire he read in her eyes. She had become like an open book to him, always sharing her thoughts and feelings, and he reveled in her honesty.

"Very well." Her deep breathy voice did not sound confident. She dropped her dressing robe upon the floor. Naked, she waited patiently as he fiddled with the last adjustments to his invention.

He had tried several times to heat the cistern of water that fed the pipe he had installed. The pipe emptied into a smaller vessel that he could pull down with a cord to dump heated water into his huge copper tub.

He reached his hand to his wife and helped her to step into the empty tub with him. "Ready?"

She giggled when he wrapped his arm around her waist. "Yes." She squeezed her eyes shut just as he pulled the cord to the bucket that dumped luxuriously heated water over them both.

"It worked!" George shouted.

"Fancy that!" Harriet kissed him soundly on the mouth. "Do it again and see what happens."

"Very well." He gave her a saucy grin. He pulled the cord and repeated the dumping of warm water. "I say, grab the soap, my love."

Giggling, she snatched a piece of soap and a soft cloth that she had ready. She then proceeded to lather his entire body.

George sighed with contentment. Harriet was everything he could have ever hoped for in a wife. Beneath the almost shy and utterly respectable surface of Miss Harriet Whitlow was a treasure chest of fire that had waited to be unlocked by him.

Never had he loved this deeply. He finally understood what it was to be cherished for always. As he in turn soaped Harriet's back, he realized that this slip of a girl, this paragon of virtue and morality had taught him a thing or two about making love.

Their union was precious and sacred. He felt as if he had been set free—finally happy and at peace. She was his and he was hers and nothing or no one would ever come between them.